Birch Blackguards

A Sutton Mass. Mystery

Lisa Shea

Cover design by Lisa Shea – the birch leaf shown came from a tree in her yard in Sutton, in autumn 2013.
Book design by Lisa Shea

This book is a work of fiction. Names, characters, places, and incidents either are products of the author's imagination or are used fictitiously. Any resemblance to actual persons, living or dead, events, or locales is entirely coincidental.

"FOLLOW THIS HIGHWAY"
Written by Holly Hanson
Performed by Neptune's Car:
Holly Hanson–vocals; Steve Hayes–background vocals, acoustic guitar, Nashville-tuned guitar, electric guitar; Sven Larson–upright bass; Mark Thayer–percussion
Courtesy of Holly Hanson
© 2010 Neptune's Car

Visit my website at SuttonMass.org

In 2014, Aspen Allegations earned a Bronze Medal from the Independent Publisher Book Awards.

First Printing: March 2014

- 5 -

Print version ISBN 978-0985556457
Kindle version ASIN B00J0L722O

Know what is right to do.
Be aware of the obstacles,
And then step up.

Birch Blackguards

Chapter 1

When you are in doubt, be still, and wait;
When doubt no longer exists for you,
    then go forward with courage.
So long as mists envelop you, be still;
be still until the sunlight pours through
and dispels the mists
    as it surely will.
Then act with courage.
~ Chief White Eagle of the Ponca Tribe (ca. 1840-1914)

Sometimes life is too much like a pathless wood, but for me, today, on this grassy patch of sun-smeared Earth, at this specific moment in time, it was the right place for love. I twined my fingers in Jason's as we stepped along the overgrown pavement, moving beneath the crumbling granite arch of the drive-in entryway. I half-suspected the dangling wires and aged stonework would collapse on our heads as we passed beneath. Against all odds the structure stayed upright, remained monumental and silent as we approached the long-abandoned triangular ticket booth and the massive screen beyond.

Jason smiled at me, his short, chestnut hair shining in the August afternoon sunlight. "So, did you ever go to drive-ins when you were a kid?"

I nodded, looking ahead to the distinctive undulating pattern of the pavement. The hills and valleys would give each car an ideal angle to the screen. The posts with speakers were long gone, though. Only the aging projection house remained, the collapsing main screen stretching before it. An assortment of spindly trees poked up through the blacktop like unruly grey hairs on a Nigerian grandfather's balding head.

I smiled as I looked across the fading scenery. "My mom would take me to the drive-in during the summers when I was young, back in the seventies. Our family had a dark green AMC Hornet. I would bring my sleeping bag and pillow and think it a grand adventure."

I shook my head, turning to the massive screen, my eyes drawn to the shadowed areas where the whiteness was interrupted by decay and collapse. Philip K. Dick would have said it was a clear sign of *kibble* – the inevitable progression of all of life into a messy chaos which smothers us.

I shrugged. "Even when I was a teenager, in the eighties, drive-ins were becoming a thing of the past. They were something seen in vintage settings, like *Grease*. My friends and I went to the multi-plexes, waiting in line for *Ghostbusters* and *Footloose*, eager for chemically-dusted popcorn and filtered air conditioning."

Jason looked over the landscape around us. "This drive-in opened back in 1947," he mused. "It survived McCarthyism, the Cold War, and Kent State. It was only the traffic patterns on 146 which finally did it in. I hear a key reason it was shut down in 1996 was that the cars backed up too much on the highway."

I let out a sigh, brushing my long, auburn hair from my face. "A shame. So much is becoming lost. Lost and decaying, while people are mesmerized by their smart phones and block out their surroundings with tiny white ear buds." My eyes drew up to the large screen, the pale squares slowly, inexorably, curling away from each other. "I wonder what they were watching back in 1947."

Jason's voice came without hesitation. "*A Gentleman's Agreement.*"

I glanced over in surprise. "Oh?"

He grinned. "My mother was an avid fan of Gregory Peck. The movie won three Academy Awards and I believe was nominated for eight."

I smiled. "Maybe we can Netflix it tonight," I offered. I looked around the wasteland. "However, right now we have a task to complete."

He nodded. "And a challenging one it is, too. Though why Jeff can't come out and track down his own gear ..."

I nudged him in the side. "We had the day free," I reminded him. "And with Citadel Airsoft being asked to stop using the grounds for their games, we need to figure out where he tucked that rifle before the new owner takes over. For all we know, they'll be bulldozing this paradise to turn it into a parking lot."

He ran a hand through his hair. "Well, so far it's gone from classic drive-in to pseudo-military combat field." His eyebrow raised. "Complete with a boat."

I followed his gaze and chuckled. Parked to the left of the projector building was a fifteen-foot motorboat. As we approached it, we could see a scattering of white pellets in its bow along with several small trees poking up through its floorboards. Apparently the opposing factions in the Battle for Sutton Drive-In had found the beached boat made for good cover.

Jason shook his head, looking around. "All right. Enough sight-seeing. Where did Jeff say he forgot this rifle of his?"

My mouth quirked up in a smile. "He didn't *forget* it," I teased him. "He *secreted* it, so he could grab it at an opportune time and sneak up on his enemy unawares." I grinned. "Then, unfortunately, he lost track of where he had put it."

I walked toward the western side of the clearing, heading away from the highway. The growl of slow cars was faintly audible in the background. It was nearly six p.m. but traffic was still backed up to the Millbury line. The legislators had talked often about removing the light at Tony's pizza, to remove this evening log-jam, but somehow nothing ever was done.

I looked at the stretch of trees before us. "Jeff said something about a stand of white birch," I commented. "There isn't anything but forest for over a half mile in this direction. Lots of options."

Jason chuckled. "Probably why the drive-in was so popular," he joked. "You know how teenagers are."

I smiled at him, and then we both dug into our pockets and pulled out leather gloves. Jason's years in the forest ranger service had made him well aware of the issues with poison ivy, poison sumac, and disease-bearing ticks. I had been dating him for just about nine months now, and I had learned quickly. No need to risk Lyme disease just to track down a plastic replica of an AR-15.

I glanced up at the sky. Earlier in the day the world had been softened by gentle showers, but now only drifting grey clouds remained, filtering the sun and adding a romantic cast to this first day of August. I took a breath and delved into the phthalo-green shadows of the forest. The landscape was different from the nearby paths in Sutton Forest and Purgatory Chasm that Jason and I enjoyed hiking. This was an overgrown tangle, once a tame edging to a family fun spot, now left to its own insidious devices. Dense patches of Virginia creeper were interlaced with gnarled stretches of goldenrod and wild strawberry.

I smiled, enjoying my explorations, keeping a sharp eye out for a straight shape amongst all the curves. Whatever the excuse, I was immensely content to be exploring the summer wilderness with Jason. His presence was a balm to me, and I had still not quite gotten used to having him in my life. Perhaps I would always hold a tinge of surprise and appreciation that he fit so easily into my world.

I certainly hoped so.

I tripped over an upturned root and went down hard on my knees into the club moss and aster. I shook my head. I wasn't elderly, but at forty-four I was hardly a toddler either. My yoga routine kept me flexible, but I respected my body's limitations. I put both hands down to press myself up off the fragrant forest floor.

My left hand settled over something smooth and cylindrical, and I smiled. Perhaps the tripping had been fate, after all. I brushed away the layer of dirt and sediment, my voice gathering to call out to Jason that I'd found the elusive weapon.

The victory cry died in my throat.

The object beneath my gloved fingers was stained with time, discolored with grime, but was clearly not a metal or plastic gun barrel. Rather, it was that delicate ivory which so clearly connected with my soul.

I stared at the bone, and time stood still.

Jason must have been calling my name, for by the time he strode over to me his face was set in half exasperation, half worry. He drew up at my side – and stopped. His gaze snapped into that serious focus that I knew so well. His hand was at his hip, he dialed the three digits, and then he dropped to one knee by my side. His arm wrapped around me, drawing me in, while he spoke into his phone.

"Jason Rowland here. I'm at the Sutton drive-in. We've found a dead body. No flesh on the bones that I can see – at least three weeks is my guess. Maybe much longer." He listened for a moment. "We'll be here."

He drew me to my feet, easing me back. I could see now the outline of the rest of the corpse. It seemed the person had been as tall as me – about five foot six – and curled onto one side. I had disturbed the femur, but the remainder remained hidden under a layer of dirt and moss. It almost seemed that a natural, earth-brown blanket comforted the dead person, nestling them in against the birch.

It was only minutes before the sirens began, before there were police officers and yellow crime-scene tape and endless questions. But I had no answers to give. The chaos came from all sides and a thought flickered in my mind. Perhaps the skeleton had been content to lie there. Perhaps we had disturbed its serene resting place with our brash, noisy intrusion.

At last the final interview was complete. I climbed in beside Jason in his white F-150 to head back home. He glanced over at me as he turned through the deepening dusk onto 146, now free flowing with light traffic. "How are you holding up?"

I rolled my shoulders. "It still doesn't seem real," I admitted. "How long had the body been there?" I looked down at my hands, pondering the sinews, the scattering of light brown freckles which made my unique constellations. "How quickly does a person go from flesh and blood to a skeleton?"

His brow furrowed, and he thought about it for a minute. "It's August first. These past few weeks have see-sawed between record heat and steady rain. Between that and summertime insect activity, in that shallow grave, full decomposition could easily have happened within the month." He looked ahead as we turned onto our street. "But it could be longer, of course. Years. Maybe decades. During the time of the drive-in's use that land would only have been visited on weekends. I imagine few of the customers ever left the pavement area." He gave a soft shrug. "For all we know, the body could even date back to before the drive-in was operational."

We drew to a stop in our driveway. He came around and took my hand, walking me up to the door. "I'm sure we'll find out more tomorrow," he assured me. "Once they start looking more closely at the bones."

Juliet, my stripy cat, was waiting for us when we opened the door, and I knelt down to pet her. I felt unsettled, lost, and I wasn't quite sure what I wanted to do.

He nodded his head to me. "Go on upstairs and settle into bed. I'll bring up some Triscuit nachos. We can watch *A Gentleman's Agreement* on Netflix. It'll keep your mind off of things and help you sleep."

I nodded and made my way upstairs. In only a few minutes he was up with the plate, as well as a glass of red sangria with frozen peaches in it. I smiled and propped up the pillows.

The movie drew me in. I had always adored *To Kill a Mockingbird*, but this showcased a different type of discrimination. It was stunning to think, so soon after the real-life horrors of Auschwitz and Dachau, that people in the US could still feel it quite reasonable to have "restricted" hotels and establishments which kept out Jews.

The movie finally spun to an end and I rolled over to look at Jason. "Even though the movie made it clear from the beginning that Phil was going to end up with Kathy, I'm not sure I like it,"

I murmured. "Throughout the courtship Kathy made disparaging remarks about Jews, even equating them to being old and sick. In comparison, Anne is honest, intelligent, and compassionate. She bares her soul to Phil and he seems to respond. Then, *poof*, Kathy makes one minor concession and he goes running right back to her."

He grinned. "Anne did win the Academy award," he pointed out, "while the rest only got nominated. So it seems others agreed with you there."

I lay against his chest. "Still, the plot is a good portrayal of how prejudice can be an insidious force. This wasn't as in-your-face as *In the Heat of the Night*, for example. Characters in this movie would not state right out that they had an issue with Jews. They would just turn away or make quiet comments."

He nodded, running a hand along my cheek. "And then we have, just today, Rhode Island accepting gay marriage with nary a rumble of an issue. Back in 2004, when Massachusetts was the first state to allow gay marriage, there was a huge outcry. Now, nearly ten years later, all of New England allows gay marriage, and life goes on, serene and content."

I held his gaze. "The world is making strides. Still, there are so many ways in which people are marginalized. Obese people are thought of as lazy. People in wheelchairs are thought of as mentally slow. When will we stop jumping to conclusions? When will we start allowing each person to shine with their natural abilities and hopes?"

He smiled at that. "They may say you're a dreamer," he murmured, "but you're not the only one."

I chuckled. "Of course not. I have you, don't I?" My throat tightened. "Every day I give thanks that you found me."

His eyes grew smoky, he drew me down to him, and the world faded away.

Chapter 2

The world glowed, saturated with rich Crayola color, as Jason and I kayaked along the eastern coastline of Manchaug Pond. The Friday evening speedboaters, pontooners, and jet-skiers were zipping back and forth across the center of the 380-acre oval. A pair of fishing boats was stationed by the sandbar in the center, taking a break under the stunning blue skies. The water itself was a luxurious cobalt blue, and all around were shimmering shades of green in a thousand different hues.

I breathed in deeply, watching as a large dragonfly flitted by, nearly the size of a dachshund. "Thank you, Jason. This is exactly what I needed."

He grinned. "I thought you might enjoy a day looking for egrets. And besides, I wanted to take this thing out and see if it leaked."

We had been out on Cape Cod the previous weekend, picking up a used Trident Predator 13 kayak he'd found on CraigsList. It was muted orange, and its rudder helped it to track well in rougher weather. In evidence of the six degrees of separation theory, the kayak's owner had previously lived in Sutton, working right across the street from Tony's Pizza.

I gently paddled past a trio of mallard ducks snoozing on a deserted dock. "And? Do you like your Trident?"

He nodded. He deftly paddled a tight circle around my kayak, a sunrise-colored Venus 11 in hues of tangerine, crimson, and golden yellow. "Good maneuverability."

He came back in position on my left side, staying attentively between me and the over-exuberant racers who almost seemed to joust with each other in bursts of spray and wave. He kept a careful eye on them as we continued our way counter-clockwise around the rim.

I looked forward toward the northwest edge of the lake, where the land sloped up a long hill to Waters Farm at the summit. "I'm still amazed that the lake association was able to hold off that large development that was moving in. Holy Cross could have turned that entire swath of natural forest into buildings."

Jason nodded. "That Beaton Farm land was incredibly important to local wildlife. It's nearly a hundred acres, between the Sutton land and that in Douglas. Now that the area has been bought and protected, the streams and forests can continue to support a rich array of species."

"The Manchaug Association almost didn't raise the money necessary to buy the land," I mused. "But at the last minute – only two weeks ago – an anonymous donor provided nearly two million dollars for the land purchase." I smiled. "If anyone deserves an enormous gold star, that donor does." I swirled my paddle in the water. "How does one give thanks to an unknown benefactor?"

His eyes twinkled. "You treat every person you meet with kindness. For you never know which one of them might be that very person."

My heart sung. Every day presented fresh opportunities for me to be warmed by his glow. My voice was rough when I spoke. "You are just right," I murmured, and it was not just his statement about kindness which had tapped my wells of emotions. I looked at the rippling maples and pines along the shoreline, continuing, "I suppose, you being a ranger and all, it comes with the territory. You, more than most, understand how important it is to preserve the untouched spaces."

He nodded, following my gaze. "Our land wasn't given to us by our parents," he murmured. "It was only leant to us by the next generation. It's our duty to treasure our natural resources, and to keep them safe for all of our future."

A pair of needle-fine blue dragonflies fluttered to rest on the tip of his kayak, acting jointly as a living figurehead, and my smile stretched through my soul.

The kayaking excursion was serenely beautiful, and I felt the afterglow of it for the full car ride back. Jason was just turning my Forester into our driveway when his cell phone rang.

"Jason here."

He listened, nodding his head, and after a short while he said, "All right. Thanks. Talk to you tomorrow."

I raised an eyebrow.

He looked at the stretch of tiger lilies waving along the end of the driveway. Then he turned to me, his gaze weary. "They have preliminary results on the body we found. It was a girl, probably around sixteen years old."

The bucolic mood from the beautiful afternoon flickered away like a morning fog hit by those first strong rays of a summer sunrise. "Do they know who she is?"

He shook his head. "They still don't know if the body lay there for ten weeks or ten years. It'll take them a while to narrow down the details." His mouth gave a dry quirk. "Not quite like on TV."

"They can't just look up dental records?"

"We need to know which dentist to ask," he pointed out. "And doctors are only required to keep records for seven years, here in Massachusetts. So depending on how long she's been in the ground, the records could be long gone." His brow creased. "Hospitals hold onto records for thirty years, so we might have more luck there, depending on what they find."

"I'm sure they'll figure it out," I murmured.

Still, as soon as I got inside, I went to my office and settled down before the inlaid desk. I googled "missing children Massachusetts."

I'm not sure what I was expecting. However, when I landed on the website for the National Center for Missing and Exploited Children, I was surprised that it only had forty-six records found for the state. Maybe this was just for this month? But no – the entries shown stretched back to children missing from 1976. Twenty-two of the children listed were tagged as runaways.

I went to the Massachusetts state website to double-check. They gave the exact same information.

How could this be? Just four days ago, all the news sites were trumpeting about a massive "Operation Cross Country" which had sought to rescue children caught in sexual slavery. They had freed over a hundred children in just that one weekend. Three of the kids had been from Boston.

I searched for the list of the Operation Cross Country results. New Haven, Connecticut had seen five children rescued during the operation. But the Missing Children website only listed seventeen children missing in the entire state of Connecticut. Had the police really tracked down a full third of all missing kids?

The Missing Children website claimed a 97% recovery rate of listed kids – which seemed fairly amazing. Did that mean the forty-six children in Massachusetts were merely the remaining few who couldn't be found? That the rest had been safely, quickly recovered?

Baffled, I did some more digging. Ah, a report by the U.S. Department of Justice. They ran analysis on the nearly 1.7 million children in 1999 who either ran away or were "thrown away" – told to leave the house. For this study the DOJ didn't even include all the various family and non-family abductions that occur.

Out of these 1.7 million children, only 21% were reported to authorities.

The rest were left to fend for themselves.

I thought again of the young girl lying in her blanket of moss. Why had nobody reported her missing? Had she fled an abusive parent? Run off in a fit of teen angst?

Another mouse click chilled my heart. Young girls, out on their own, were extremely vulnerable to predators. The current average age a girl got drawn into the sex trade was a tender twelve to fourteen. There were now an estimated 300,000 girls in that tragic predicament – and only one percent of them would ever be rescued.

A hand gently rested on my shoulder. Jason's voice was laden with sadness. "Hard reading," he murmured. "This goes on every day, and most people think it's a distant problem. They figure that it happens in a far-off big city. But in our world of Facebook and online chat rooms, any lonely child can fall victim to it."

He glanced at the phone in his hand. "We may not be able to save them all, but we might be able to bring peace to just this one girl. No luck finding a missing person report?"

I shook my head. "Whoever she was, her family never reported it when she vanished. It makes me wonder why."

His eyes were shadowed. "Well then, we will be her guardian angels. It sounds like she needed one."

I smiled, looking up at him. "I would like that."

He held out the phone. "Well, then, this might be our first step. Do you recognize this? It was found near the victim's hand."

The phone image showed a ruler. Next to it was an irregularly shaped object, perhaps four inches long, mustard in color, with a lumpy, oblong shape.

I took the phone from Jason and looked more closely at the object. There was a bulbous sag to one side, and the area above it could almost be a face.

A glimmer of an idea came to me. "It looks sort of like an odd version of one of the Vaillancourt Santas."

He raised an eyebrow. "The what?"

"Vaillancourt Folk Art," I explained. "They make internationally recognized collectible figurines, and they're right here in Sutton. Everything there is hand-made. They specialize in using old chocolate molds, and they typically cast out of chalk."

He glanced out the window at the darkness beyond. "Are they open on Saturdays?"

I nodded. "Seven days a week. Interested in taking a tour with me tomorrow?"

He smiled. "Absolutely."

Chapter 3

Jason and I walked up to the entrance of the Manchaug Mills structure, looking up at the large, three-story brick building. It was located opposite from Manchaug Falls. At one time, after its incarnation as a textile mill, it had been the launching spot for a small company called Fruit of the Loom. Now it hosted a variety of offices, workshops, and, in a large suite, the Christmassy cheer of Vaillancourt Folk Art.

We went down the short hall to Vaillancourt's main door and immediately stepped into a holiday wonderland. There were shimmering Christmas trees, shelves of delicate ornaments, pedestals with Irish Santas, and display cases holding historic, one-of-a-kind creations. There were Santas with red jackets, Santas with Irish shamrocks, Santas with gold leaf, and even Santas with beach wear. There were nativity sets with rhinoceroses and giraffes, and I could see other shelves in the distance with even more fascinating objects.

We turned right, to where a dark-haired artist in his thirties was hunched over a chalk figurine, carefully applying ruby-red paint to the Santa's cloak. I waited until he saw us. "We're here to see Gary Vaillancourt."

He smiled. "Sure thing, just one minute." He picked up a phone, spoke into it, then nodded. "He'll be here shortly."

Footsteps sounded from down the hall, and Gary Vaillancourt walked toward us. He was a handsome man, greying, neatly dressed, with a ready smile. He held out his hand.

"Morgan, Jason, it is a pleasure to meet you both." We shook hands around. "Come, let us have a seat." He guided us over into another area which was set up with leather sofas and a low table. Once we had all sat down, he looked to us. "So, how can I help you? Something about an item you found?"

Jason brought up the image on his cell, and then handed it over to Gary. "Do you recognize this design?"

Gary studied the photo for a moment, turning the cell in the light to get a better angle on it. "I think so," he murmured. "Come, let me show you."

He stood and guided us down the right side of the room, to a small display case, He pointed to one of the middle shelves. Three painted Santas stood there, each about four inches high. They had traditional red coats with white fur trim and carried a deep blue sack. Each sack was painted with several gold stars and a single, larger crescent moon.

He held the phone up next to the Santas. "I think what you have is an early edition of one of these Santas. See how the bag is carried on his shoulder? This would have been our very first design, right when Judi initially received the molds."

I looked at the figurines. The red paint was lightly cracked with age, but the detail on the body, from its thin tan belt to its delicate golden buckle, was exquisite. "She really makes these with chocolate molds?"

He nodded. "I got her the first three antique molds as a present for her birthday, in April 1984. She made chocolate with them initially, of course, but then her creativity blossomed. She began experimenting with beeswax and liquid chalk, to see if she could create something more permanent. We sold them out of Waters Farm – it's a farmstead up above Manchaug Pond."

I nodded. "Yes, we were out kayaking on Manchaug just yesterday. It's a lovely area. I know Waters Farm holds oxen days in the fall."

His eyes lit up. "Did you know back in colonial days that Sutton was considered the best oxen training area in the whole colonies? Daniel Webster, who had stayed in town several times, wrote about the acclaim."

My eyes lit up. "I had no idea! I'll have to do some more reading about it."

He motioned back toward the Santas. "My wife Judi modeled this artwork on the painting done by N. C. Wyeth of 'Old Nick'. You can see those same stars and crescent moon in Wyeth's painting." He looked down at the phone again, and his eyes grew somber. "You said this had something to do with the girl found over at the Sutton drive-in?"

I nodded. "This object was found near the skeleton."

He shook his head. "A sad thing. I hope they determine who she was and what happened to her." His brow creased. "If she had been in the elements long enough to turn into a skeleton, a chalkware Santa would have completely dissolved away. Chalkware is made from gypsum. It would turn to a mush in water."

He looked again at the cell phone image, his eyes focusing in. "Perhaps ... I wonder if this could be the beeswax figure she made for the First Congregational Church commemoration in 1984."

I raised an eyebrow. "What was that for?"

"The church had a tragedy occur in 1828 – their building burned down. The reverend at the time was John Maltby. He rallied the congregation's hopes and gently shepherded them until they could get their new building constructed – the one on the town common this very day. Maltby then cared for his flock until 1834. The church was commemorating the 150th anniversary of his stewardship."

He turned back to the figurines on the shelf. "My wife was just getting started with her project in 1984, but when the church asked if she could donate something, she offered one of her beeswax versions. It has to be that Santa. There's no way it could have lasted the elements otherwise."

Jason looked between us. "I thought beeswax had a low melting point?"

Gary nodded. "About 150°F, but if this unfortunate girl was laid to rest in the shadows of a forest I wouldn't think that to be a problem."

I looked to Jason. "My good friend Joan goes to the First Congregational Church, to the Sunday 10 a.m. service. I can ask to go with her tomorrow and see if they kept any records about the raffle. Maybe they know who won that piece. I could find out if this is related somehow."

He nodded to me. "That sounds like a good idea. I'll let the police know, too, that we think we might have identified the object for them. I'm sure they can do more precise tests to verify that it really is what we think it is."

Gary waved a hand. "Would you like to see the workshop while you are here?"

My eyes lit up. "Absolutely!"

He guided us down the center area of the shop, back toward where we had met the artist when we first came in. We turned right into a room about the size of my living room. There were rows and rows of shelves on the back wall, each holding a myriad of antique metal molds of all shapes and sizes.

He motioned at the molds. "This is where it all begins," he explained. "We use these actual, authentic, original molds for each item we create. We have to do this by hand, one at a time. We set up a mold, pour in the liquid chalk, and then it takes a full three days for the chalk to dry. Next comes the sanding, then a white paint layer, then a base coat. And that is all before the artist can begin his or her work."

He brought us back out to the artist stations. "We work with oil paints, so the designs have to go on in layers. It can take three weeks before a given piece is complete. Zach here has been with us for seventeen years, and we have some artists who have been doing this with us for twenty-seven years. It is absolutely a labor of love; a family affair."

I looked up at the shelves of finished figurines. The variety of shapes was stunning, and each figurine seemed to have its own personality. "They are gorgeous."

"Thank you." He looked back toward the couches. "Did you want to sit and talk some more?"

I shook my head. "We've taken up enough of your time – I'm sure you're busy with many things. Thank you so much for talking with us."

He smiled. "My pleasure."

Jason and I walked back out to his F-150 and I was dialing my cell as I settled into the seat. "Joan? It's Morgan."

"Morgan! It's lovely to hear from you."

"Were you planning on going to church for 10 a.m. tomorrow? If so, could I come along?"

I could hear her smile across the airwaves. "Absolutely, I would be delighted. I can meet you in the parking lot at 9:50 a.m. How does that sound?"

"That would be just lovely."

Her voice took on a somber note. "I heard about you and Jason at the drive-in. I'm so sorry."

"Hopefully we can bring the girl some peace," I murmured.

"And to think of all the times I've been there," she mused, her voice unsettled. "My mother adored that place. I'm sure I went every weekend growing up. She was even there when it first opened in 1947. Some sort of a film about Jewish discrimination."

"*A Gentleman's Agreement*," I responded, looking over to Jason. "We watched it last night on Netflix."

"No, no, that was the one with Gregory Peck," she countered. "It was another one."

I furrowed my brow. "Surely there weren't two movies both about Jewish discrimination in 1947?"

"Yes," she stated, "and in fact both were nominated for best motion picture. *Gentleman's Agreement* won – but ... ah! *Crossfire*. *Crossfire* earned its own acclaim with audiences."

I looked over at Jason. "Thank you, Joan. Maybe Jason and I will have to watch that tonight."

"Sounds good. See you tomorrow morning."

I spent the afternoon catching up on dishes and decluttering, and by the time evening rolled around I was quite ready to curl up in bed with an interesting movie. As it turned out Netflix didn't have *Crossfire* in its system at all – but Amazon Prime had it available to watch instantly.

I shook my head, glancing at Jason as the black and white RKO logo flickered on the TV. "How did people live in the old days? If they wanted to watch something, they had to hope against hope that one of the three big networks might eventually decide to run it. Then they had to rearrange their work and life schedule around it, to be in front of the TV at that exact moment!"

He grinned, giving me a fond kiss on the forehead. "I know. I can't fathom how people could live with such immense difficulties."

I gently elbowed him in the ribs, and we settled in to watch.

Crossfire was intriguingly different from *Gentleman's Agreement*, with both being made in the exact same year, on the exact same topic. *Gentleman's Agreement* was about those who were supposedly above violence and harsh language. The characters by and large were upper class and educated. They would never openly attack each other over religion. Instead, they couched their prejudices behind unspoken rules and subtle innuendos. Many of the characters who thought they were not biased at all did in fact hold bias which they were unable to see.

In comparison, *Crossfire* was about a different segment of society – the working class / soldier level. These men were rough and tumble and were not above mixing it up with fists if the mood struck them. It was considered fairly normal for one of them – Montgomery – to throw bullying statements at half the people around him. A fellow soldier from Nebraska was a *hillbilly*, while Samuel, the stranger he met in the bar, was a *lazy Jew*. Montgomery assumed Samuel weaseled his way out of army service – when in fact Samuel had been injured at Okinawa.

I curled up against Jason as the movie came to an end. "I think the police investigator had it right," I murmured. "Hate is like a loaded gun. If you carry it with you too long, it can be set off by an innocent person. It shows again why it's so important to dispel hatred, especially this kind of mindless group-wide discrimination."

He ran his hand down my hair. "Even more intriguing – *Crossfire* was based on a book written by Marine Sergeant Richard Brooks, and it was originally about homosexuality. In the 1940s a movie couldn't be made about such a taboo subject, so they 'softened' it to only talk about the pervasive issues of anti-semitism."

I shook my head. "Samuel's character was right. It seems sometimes that some people have fear and hate built up within them and they simply seek targets to aim it at. For a while it was the Irish, then Catholics, then Jews, then blacks, then gays. Will we ever get to a point where we can release this hate and simply accept each other as fellow travelers on this planet we call Earth?"

I looked into his eyes. "We have such a brief time here. A blink of an eye and it's over. Surely we can be kind to each other for such a short journey and wish each other well."

He gently smiled, brushing a lock of hair from my cheek. "You'll be a swinger of birches for some time yet, climbing their swaying branches, reaching for the stars, while staying grounded here on earth."

"You ground me," I murmured. "I know you'll catch me if I fall."

He brushed his lips against mine, his gaze smoky. "I absolutely will."

And then we were lost.

Chapter 4

Joan was waiting for me in the parking lot of the First Congregational Church, looking out at the butterflies dancing across the town green. The morning sun glistened off the common's white gazebo, giving it a warm shimmer. Joan was in her sixties, white haired, with a friendly smile and warm heart.

She turned as I approached. "Good morning! Ready for service?"

I nodded, smoothing down my moss-green dress. "Yes, indeed."

We headed into the building. Although over a hundred years old, it was fresh and clean, with an entry area opening up into the main chamber. We were each handed a small pamphlet containing the day's service information, then continued in.

On each side of the center aisle were two sets of pews, a lovely combination of white with natural wood. The ceiling was painted in robin's egg blue, with ivory plaster holding the chandelier. The stained glass down the side was done with a golden theme, sending gentle light into the room.

I took my place in a pew with Joan, then looked to the front of the room. A pair of stained glass windows flanked a podium. The right scene portrayed Jesus, while the left showed this church we were in nestled into the rolling hills of Sutton. There was an apple tree, sheaves of wheat, and a farmer carefully tending to his field.

I smiled. I liked the warm atmosphere the church presented. It felt comfortable, approachable, as if all would be welcome.

The service was lovely. The congregation sang several hymns, the choir sang to us, and we engaged in call-and-response with the reverend. She was a middle-aged woman with short auburn hair and a warm smile. Her outfit, a brown tunic over pants, was neat while also seeming like something one's friends would wear.

She talked to us of the challenging nature of life, how it is by weathering the smaller storms that we build the strength to handle the larger ones. She talked about developing deep roots which could sustain us through the many hurdles life throws at us.

When the service was complete, we headed into the basement for coffee and conversation. The reverend made her rounds and eventually came to where Joan and I stood.

Joan made a hand motion in my direction. "Reverend, this is a friend of mine, Morgan."

The reverend put out her hand. "Welcome, Morgan. It's always lovely to see a fresh face here."

I smiled at her. "I enjoyed the service immensely. Especially where we drew inspiration from the hummingbirds and sunflowers."

She nodded. "All of nature can bring us closer to what is important in life."

"I agree wholeheartedly." I glanced at Joan before continuing. "I hope you don't mind, but I also have a question. It involves some research I'm doing into the poor girl who was found at the drive-in."

Her eyes shadowed. "I heard about that. Certainly, how can I help you?"

"Back in 1984, during your 150 year celebration, you raffled off a number of items. One of them was a rare first-run piece made by Judi Vaillancourt. It was a beeswax version of her very first Santa."

Her brow creased. "That was long before my time," she mused. "Still, I could go look through the records. It seems unlikely that they would have kept track of something like that, but you never know."

A portly man in a striped polo shirt stepped over. His grey hair was slightly askew, as if wind-tossed, and his wrinkled face was kind. "The 150th? That was quite a festival. Early June –

we'd had quite a storm come through and trees were down everywhere. Yes, yes, I remember that well."

The reverend turned to him. "Do you happen to remember who won the beeswax figurine from Vaillancourt?"

He nodded. "Oh, certainly. It was so odd. It was that boy from the Pleasant Valley Country Club. The caddie. He was nearly out of high school by then and was always the quiet type. Studious. But when he won that Santa figurine, it was as if he won the largest lottery prize ever. He was whooping and hollering the whole way down the aisle." He chuckled. "Never seen anything like it. I guess that boy really must have liked Christmas."

My heart rose. "Do you remember his name?"

He looked up to the ceiling as he thought. "Was it Zach? Zed? Zeke? It was something like that. Flaming red hair, I recall. He was a good caddy. Paid attention to details."

I looked between the two. "Does he still attend the church?"

The man shook his head. "Don't recall seeing him after he graduated. Figure he went off to college somewhere. You know how kids are. Eager to get out of their sleepy home town, to go off and experience the wide world. His family moved on as well – to Ohio or somewhere."

"I suppose I can go ask at Pleasant Valley," I mused. "Thank you both so much for your time." I turned to Joan. "And thank you for allowing me to come to the service with you. It was lovely."

She nodded. "Good luck with your research."

I headed out to my car and had my phone at my ear as I turned onto Boston Road. "Jason? How would you like lunch on the patio of Pleasant Valley?"

I heard the smile in his voice. "The sun is shining, the birds are singing, and we get to spend time together with good food? Count me in." His voice lowered. "I did get some news, though. They are sure the girl's body was in the ground for at least twenty years, based on the bones' decay. They're still working on narrowing the range further."

My heart fell at the thought of this girl missing for twenty long years with nobody looking for her. Why had she been abandoned?

"Thank you. See you soon."

Twenty minutes later we were taking a seat at a table overlooking the course. The sky was an odd mixture of moods, with half streaming sunshine and the other half greying with clouds. I looked up at the swirling. "I wonder which one is going to win?"

The waitress came by. "Welcome! What would you like today?"

"I'll have the wild mushroom ravioli with a side salad. Ranch. And a chardonnay, please."

Jason looked up. "Are your onion rings any good?"

She nodded. "They're delicious."

He smiled. "All right, then. Onion rings and water with lemon."

"Coming right up!"

We settled back in our chairs, watching the movement of the clouds. The tug-of-war was slowly sliding in favor of the grey billows.

Blaaare!

A loud air-horn sounded from the right hand side, and I looked over to Jason in confusion.

The sound came again, and he looked to the sky. "They've seen lightning," he explained. "They're calling all the golfers in."

A thirty-something man in a pale green polo shirt came walking across the front of the practice green, carrying an air horn. He went to the far left of the patio area and sounded the horn again in that direction.

Sure enough, like ducklings running for the safety of their mother, a stream of carts poured up the slope and pulled into a stop beneath the overhang. The skies opened up and heavy drops of rain pattered in steady tattoo against the practice green. In short order the tables were filled with laughing golfers ordering drinks and appetizers, quite content to pass the short while before the sun reappeared again.

Our waitress arrived with our food, and I offered Jason one of my ravioli.

"Delicious," he murmured, before starting in on his onion rings.

I took a bite of the ravioli, along with a few of the green beans. It was, indeed, quite flavorful.

The air-horn man came by us again, this time carrying a watering can. He began tending to each of the hanging baskets of petunias along the length of the patio.

A booming voice sounded from behind me. "Morgan! And Jason!"

I turned with a smile. Richard stood there, his crimson polo shirt neat, a glass of what I guessed to be a vodka-and-tonic in one hand. We had first met the gregarious lawyer last fall, and, Sutton being as small as it was, we had run into him a few times in various locations in the intervening months.

Richard plunked himself down into one of our chairs, taking a sip of his drink. "The storm will be past in no time," he advised. "Still, it's always nice to come in and get refreshed. How are you two doing?"

I smiled. "Doing well, thank you."

He waved a hand at the patio. "It's good to see you here. Not many locals realize that the restaurant is open to non-members. Pleasant Valley has good food; it's a shame to see it not taken advantage of."

I nodded. "Actually, we came here to find something out."

He raised an eyebrow. "Oh? Something about the teenage girl that was found at the drive-in? So far it doesn't seem they've narrowed down the precise year she died or who she was."

I shook my head at the information network which seemed to flourish in town. Richard was certainly tapped into it.

"I had a question about one of the caddies here at Pleasant Valley."

He laughed out loud. "We haven't had those in, what, twenty years? The poor kids were driven out by carts and automation." He shook his head. "And we called it progress. Can't chat with a cart, can you." He took a pull on his drink.

"No, no," I explained, "This would have been a while ago. Probably 1980 to 1983, that time frame. A red-head kid named Zeke or Zed or something like that."

Richard's eyes lit up. "Xander! Oh sure, the kid was a legend. Quiet, attentive, and he knew exactly what to recommend. I always asked for him."

Hope lit my heart. "Do you know what college he went to?"

He shook his head. "Xander never went to college. He graduated from high school and lost all drive to do anything else. He got in and out of trouble and fired from a few jobs." He shrugged. "Happens to some men. I see him fishing down off the Lake Singletary boat ramp most weeknights, when I take my boat out." His look softened. "After your efforts last fall, I finally got myself a boat. I go out, sometimes, with Charles and Sam. We drift around the lake and talk. It soothes the soul."

I smiled. "I'm glad you three are spending time together again."

He nodded, then his brow creased. "You don't think Xander had anything to do with this girl's death?"

I shook my head. "He just came up in a long tangent," I assured him. "I'm sure he's just one link in a twisted chain. If this even relates at all."

"That's good to hear. He seemed a good lad, at least when he was younger." He finished off his drink. "Now, well, at least he has his fishing. It doesn't seem like he has much else going for him."

The sun burst through the clouds, and I half expected a rainbow to shimmer across the clearing sky.

Richard looked up. "Well, that's my cue. Good luck with your investigations."

"Thank you again," I responded.

He strode over to his cart, hopped in, and in a moment he was streaming off toward his game.

I turned to look at Jason. "I know we were thinking of kayaking at Whitehall Reservoir this afternoon, but maybe we could swing by Singletary on the way?"

He nodded. "Absolutely."

In a short while we were driving up 146 North toward the Millbury side of Singletary. I shook my head as we passed a large billboard proclaiming, "Attention Sutton Residents. Troopers are your Best Protection." I turned to Jason. "Did you read about that?

He glanced up at the sign, raising an eyebrow. "Best protection from what?"

I grinned. "The Telegram had a big piece about it on their website today. Apparently that construction on 146 is finally going to go through this fall – and it involves a fair amount of police detail and overtime. The reporter said it would bring a 'major new source of extra money' for whoever could claim it."

His mouth quirked into a smile. "Seems like money can stir things up just about anywhere. So 146, being a highway and not quite an interstate, falls into murky waters?"

I nodded. "Apparently it's usually shared between the staties and the local cops. The staties handle the fatalities, while the locals handle the minor fender benders. So, with the upcoming traffic details, Sutton assumed they'd share that as well." My grin widened. "The staties had other ideas. They wanted it all for themselves."

His eyebrows drew together. "They seem to be feeling that way in other areas as well. I know there were some issues over at Purgatory, with it being a state property. The staties wanted to handle looking for lost hikers who call for help, even though the locals have the equipment to track down the cell phone location."

I sighed. "I suppose it's like one sees on TV shows all the time. Different levels of the system conflict with each other, and few end up happy. The locals get pushed aside by the staties, and the staties get pushed aside by the FBI. But in the end, the FBI and staties go back to their distant headquarters, and it's the locals who have to live there every day. They are the ones who have the ultimate responsibility."

He nodded, then turned. I looked up – we were at Singletary. A young boy was fishing from the dock, and a small fishing boat was being lowered into the water.

Jason looked at me. "Did you want to hang around for a while?"

I shook my head. "It sounded like he wasn't around weekends anyway," I pointed out. "We could come back here and kayak tomorrow. You wanted Whitehall, so Whitehall it is."

We headed east, and Jason hit the play button on his stereo. Soon we were singing along with Neptune's Car –

Follow this highway
Through the canyon where the red rocks glow
Wind through the forest
Trace the rim edge where the pine trees grow.

I smiled at Jason. "They're out touring in Michigan. Hopefully they'll be back soon. I love to hear them live. They're such a delight."

He nodded. "And my band has that benefit on the tenth."

I grinned. "I'll definitely be there."

In short order we were sliding the kayaks into the water. We glided out into the quiet lake, side by side, through the swaths of lily pads. Whitehall didn't allow skiers or fast travel, which meant there were only a few kayakers across the way and three small fishing boats in the far distance. We could explore in peace.

I breathed in the serenity as we eased past a great blue heron and laughed in delight at the antics of a dancing dragonfly.

I looked at all the closed buds of the water lilies as we paddled along the shore. "Someday we'll have to make it out here in the morning, when these are all blooming," I mused. "We always get them when they're closed."

His brow quirked up. "I think the only way you'll be awake in the morning is to stay up overnight," he pointed out. "You were barely able to manage that 10 a.m. service this morning."

I grinned. "Ah, but I did it!" I pointed out. "So sometime, before the summer is through, maybe I can achieve a morning kayak run."

He made a flourishing gesture with his hand. "If you wake up, I will definitely be there at your side."

I smiled at him, the sun shimmered golden off the mirror-smooth surface, and my soul was at peace.

.

Chapter 5

We drove up Route 146 North past the blaring billboard, *TROOPERS ARE YOUR BEST PROTECTION*, and I shook my head. I certainly wasn't going to call State Troopers if a burglar broke into my house. It hadn't been State Troopers who had noticed an out-of place car behind the Bank of America about a month back and had been able to thwart a potential robbery. It had been the Sutton police chief, born and raised in Sutton, intimately aware of its ins and outs.

We came off 146 at West Main in Millbury, and in short order we were pulling into the Singletary boat ramp parking lot. A middle-aged woman with a long, dark ponytail was keeping an eye on four boys who looked to be about twelve. Two were fishing from the boat ramp, while another two were paddling around with rods in an inflatable raft. There were no other fishermen in sight.

Jason looked over at me. "Shall we meander around for a while and see who shows up?"

I smiled. "Absolutely."

In under ten minutes we were gliding along in the water.

It was one of those beautiful *no cloud in the sky* days, and the sky's blue was an exact match for the ceiling of the First Congregational Church. All it needed was a white plaster round with a chandelier hanging from it. And perhaps a song or two.

I sang in time with my strokes.

*"Follow this highway
Through the canyon where the red rocks glow"*

Jason smiled at me. "Seems fitting – Neptune's Car was a clipper ship in the 1800s, captained by a female." He looked at my kayak. "Yours is a bit smaller, perhaps, but the same idea."

I glanced up at the brim of my hat and then grinned, carefully removing my hat from my head. "And look! I even have a first mate."

It was a delicate, lime-green katydid with a long, curved tail. Jason examined it for a moment while it daintily cleaned its antennae with its front feet. "I do think you have a drumming katydid there. They're a relatively recent arrival from Europe. Apparently you have an international crew on that boat of yours."

I gently reseated my hat on my head and looked along the shoreline. My eyes lit up. "We may not have glowing red rocks along this watery highway of ours, but the water level is so high that there's actually a passable way through this section! The isthmus has become submerged! Our very own Panama Canal."

He shook his head, looking at the area. "If that is passable, it will be by inches," he murmured. "That jumble of rocks is barely beneath the surface."

His eyes lifted to mine, and he shook his head again, smiling. "But you are determined, so I will head in first."

He turned the nose of his kayak, carefully threading his way amongst the boulders and reeds. I followed attentively behind him. A final push, and we were through on the other side.

I raised both hands in the air. "Victory! We are explorers!"

He chuckled, then hung back so I could take the lead. I smiled. He knew this would give me the best opportunity to get as close as possible to the delicate blue dragonflies, the trio of sleeping ducks, and the shimmering sunfish before they eased from our presence.

I took a sip of water as the ducks paddled away. "Do they always come in threes? I would think twos made more sense."

He quirked an eyebrow. "Maybe they keep a spare around, as a backup."

I turned on him in mock solemnity. "Don't you even think about it."

He raised his hands in surrender. "I am more than content with one," he promised.

I grinned. "Good."

We followed the edge of the lake, moving past countless silent houses, their docks empty, their deck chairs abandoned. I shook my head. If I lived on the lake, I would be out there every day, soaking in the beauty of the water, the gentle paddling of the ducks. I wondered if some people became inured to the landscape, came to think of it as a wall painting – something taken for granted and barely seen. It would be the fine china - featured for a weekend party with friends, and then tucked away into a drawer.

There was a movement from high above, and I tracked it with my eyes. "Look! An osprey!"

The bird was beautiful, with its white head and dark body, and it circled leisurely across the robin's egg blue sky. I gazed after it.

Crunch.

I looked down in surprise. My kayak had run right into a downed tree, and sprawling dead branches were all about me. To my right, a large spider's web shimmered in the breeze. Eight round eyes placidly gazed at me.

I laughed in delight. "Apparently I should watch where I am going," I teased Jason, carefully backing out of the tree. "I'm responsible for this delicate little katydid, and I'm about to serve her up for lunch!"

He watched with amusement as I untangled myself and followed behind him. We moved along a low stone wall, and several small sunfish followed along after me. I wondered if they had a hankering for katydid and took care not to move my head quickly. My little friend perched contentedly on my brim, like a figurehead, apparently enjoying her drifting vantage spot.

There was a long, thick, knotted rope dangling from a leaning tree ahead – apparently youngsters enjoyed swinging from it and launching into the water. I gazed up at it as I approached it. There was a two-inch-diameter branch tied mid-way up the rope, perhaps to be used as a handle of sorts. The branch looked near the point of disintegration. Surely it couldn't be safe to –

Crunch.

This time I laughed out loud. Somehow I had managed to ground myself on a large, flat rock. Jason grinned as he came over to me and gently tugged me backwards off of it.

I shook my head. "OK, I think I get the message," I sighed. "No looking up for long periods of time while kayaking."

"It does help to watch what's before you," he agreed. His eyes scanned forward, to the boat ramp. "Speaking of which …"

I followed his gaze. A man in his late forties, wearing a rumpled grey t-shirt and cut-off jeans, was settling down at the edge of the parking lot, where it abutted Singletary. He picked up his rod and cast it out into the water.

Jason looked at me, and I nodded. We paddled our way back to the boat ramp and loaded the kayaks and gear back into my Forester. Then we strolled over to the man.

His hair was dark brown, greying, and his skin held a deep tan. His face was weathered, with frown lines carved into his cheeks. The faint aroma of rum came off of him. He passively stared out at the water, his shoulders slumping.

Jason spoke while looking out at the water. "I hear the pumpkinseed are biting."

The man nodded. "Yup. Bluegills too."

"Do you ever go out on the water?"

He shook his head. "Nope. Just fish from shore. Can't swim."

"Never too late to learn, you know."

The man almost smiled. "My mother tried to teach me, over at Marion's Camp," he stated, nudging his head vaguely south. "It didn't take. I'm fine with the shore."

"So you grew up here? A nice town."

He shrugged. "Has its ups and downs, like any place. But all and all, I like it. The rolling hills. The nooks. It feels comfortable, like a worn-in slipper."

Jason put out his hand. "I'm Jason. Morgan and I live in Sutton, over on the west side."

The man put his rod into his left hand, holding out his right. "I'm Xander. I have an apartment here, near the center of town. Small, but it gets the job done."

Jason's phone buzzed, and he looked down with a frown. He glanced at the screen, then looked at me. "There's a trail issue in Sutton Forest and they need a hand with it."

I nodded. "Of course." I flicked my eyes toward Xander.

Jason turned to him. "I have been wanting to get into fishing for years," he mused, "but I didn't know where to begin. I don't suppose you'd be up for meeting at West End Creamery tomorrow, to chat a bit? My treat, of course."

Xander's eyes lit up. "We used to go there all the time, when I was young," he murmured. "It's right by Swans Pond. They have the best ice cream." He looked up at us. "That'd be nice. Maybe at six, before I start fishing?"

Jason put out his hand, smiling. "It's a deal. I look forward to talking."

Xander shook the hand, then nodded at me. His eyes had a little more sparkle to them as he looked back out at the water.

I climbed into the Forester with Jason, and we headed south. After a few minutes Jason looked over at me. "I imagine you'd rather not wait another day, but –"

I smiled. "Not to worry. You take care of your duties, and I'll continue my research. If Xander really did win that beeswax Santa, and somehow that Santa got to the dead girl, then that means she died sometime after spring 1984. So that at least narrows the window down further. Sometime between 1984 and 1993, it seems."

He pulled into our driveway, gave me a kiss, then swapped over to his F-150. In a moment he was down the road and gone.

I gathered up my laptop and went out onto the back porch, looking over at the square which held the green remnants of the day lilies. Every year I looked forward to their bright orange flowers – and every year it seemed all too soon before they had finished their run for the season. I wondered what the swallowtail butterflies had moved on to. They seemed so blissful when delving deep into the day lily's tangerine nectar.

My previous quests on the missing children websites had been fruitless. Maybe another approach would work better? I decided to tackle local newspaper archives, to see if any of them discussed missing teenage girls. I spread my range to Providence, to Boston, and to Springfield. Route 146 was, after all, a connector road between Worcester and Providence. Maybe she had been en route from one place to another when fate cut her life short.

By the time Jason got home again I was curled up on the couch, Juliet nestled at my side. I looked up. "Welcome home."

He looked over as he closed the door behind him. "Any luck?"

I shook my head. "It seems a missing child is rarely considered important news. The few times it gets brought up, there is some sort of a resolution to it fairly quickly." I shook my head. "With all the children that go missing, don't the parents care?"

Jason's eyes shadowed. "It was only five days ago that news broke of a game show in Pakistan where contestants win actual, human babies as prizes." His lips formed a thin line. "They're handed out like a stuffed animal or a Kewpie doll."

I closed the laptop screen, standing and moving to draw him into a hug. "We'll bring rest for this one," I murmured to him. "We'll make a difference in this one case."

He pressed a kiss onto my forehead. "Just one starfish at a time."

My heart warmed, and I nodded. "One starfish at a time."

Chapter 6

West End Creamery is perhaps two inches from the Sutton-Whitinsville line, just down the road from Purgatory Chasm. The sky was full of those gorgeously fluffy white clouds that painters dream about, and the beautiful weather had drawn out every child for miles. The miniature golf course had tiny golfers on every green, the Barnyard Jump bouncy area was leaping with life, and nearly all of the picnic tables had smiling families enjoying ice cream and other treats.

Jason and I stepped from the bright outdoors into the large barn, and it took a moment for my eyes to adjust. I was surprised that there was nobody in sight – just us and the contentedly snoozing animals. "Guess we're the only ones drawn to the quieter pursuits today," I teased him before walking over to the large chicken coop. I smiled. "Not that I mind," I added. "I'm happy to have these beauties all to myself."

He watched my eyes for a moment before gently shaking his head. "No, not a good idea."

I raised my eyebrows at him.

"You want chickens," he expanded. "I know about your dreams. But chickens like these Rhode Island Reds can leave life at only four years. I know how upset you were when your parakeet, Ivory, passed away last month. And she was twelve. Can you imagine having a whole flock of chickens that you adored and having them become seriously ill after only a few years? You'd be living at the vet's with your feathery chickens under each arm."

I sighed, watching the fluffy little creatures amble around their enclosure. "But they are so cute!"

He waved a hand. "And we can come visit them every week, if you wish. Your own private little flock."

I nodded. We moved on to the goats and the darling pair of alpaca. Jason grinned at the chocolate brown one. "Now he looks like he'd be nice to cuddle with. Look at that fur. I bet it's soft."

My eyes lit up, and he laughed. "I can only imagine what the neighbors would have to say about that."

We spent a few more minutes with the rabbits and calves before heading back out to the entryway. At six on the dot Xander pulled into the parking lot in a light blue Oldsmobile which had clearly seen better days. The front quarter was rusting through and there was an impressive dent in the driver's door.

He came over to join us, seemingly in the same grey t-shirt and cut-off jeans as yesterday. The aroma of rum wafted along with him.

Jason put out his hand. "Hey there, Xander, so glad you could join us. Jason and Morgan, in case you forgot."

Xander tapped his head. "Didn't forget. Everything gets stored in there."

Jason waved a hand. "All right, then. Shall we order?"

We joined the lines, and I stared at the myriad of options listed on the board.

When we reached the counter, I leant forward to the teen girl waiting in the window. "A medium chocolate-vanilla twist with jimmies," I stated.

"Cone or cup?"

"Cone, please."

The girl's eyes moved to Jason. "For you?"

He shook his head. "Nothing for me." He motioned to Xander.

"A large sundae with chocolate chip ice cream. Add some Nerds to that too."

Jason handed over a ten, and the girl gave him back the change. "Coming right up!" She slid the glass window shut.

I gazed at the large-scale model train perched above the top of the window on an elevated track. "Look, that is so cool!"

Jason smiled. "You and trains," he murmured.

I shrugged. "I like them! Someday we'll go on a train ride across Canada and it will be sheer bliss."

The window slid open again and our ice cream was handed out. I took a lick as we headed over to a table with a dark green umbrella. Swan Pond glistened before us in the sunshine.

Jason motioned with his head. "Ever fished here, Xander?"

He shook his head, eagerly taking in a large spoonful of the sundae as if it was his first meal of the day. "Nah. I stick to Singletary. You can't fish from the Manchaug boat ramp. Used to fish at the Carpenter Reservoir sometimes, but then they made that off limits too."

I nodded, licking around the cone, creating a delicious combination of jimmies and twisting chocolate-plus-vanilla. "I know. I used to kayak there. Suddenly there were giant boulders blocking the parking lot and no trespassing signs."

His eyes lit up. "You were hit by that too? What were they thinking? It used to be a decent world. You do your day's work, you go to the pond, you fish. Now it's all rules and regulations." He reached into his hip pocket and pulled out a flask, taking a nip of it. "Rules and regulations."

Jason glanced at me, his face steady, before returning to look at Xander. "So, how long have you been fishing?"

He smiled at that. "Ah, since I was just a little tyke. Grew up digging for worms and using them to pull pumpkinseed sunfish out of Singletary. You'd find me there most evenings. That was my life. Golf in the day, sunfish at night."

"Oh, so you're a golfer? Where did you play?"

He nudged his head north. "Up at Pleasant Valley. Not that I could afford it, especially not in those days, back when the PGA was playing there." His eyes dropped. "It was a sad day when that ended in 1998. Trouble with finding sponsors and drawing in the crowds. I guess Sutton was just too quiet for the big city folk."

Jason leant forward. "If you couldn't afford it, how were you playing there?"

Xander took another scoop. "I was a caddy in high school. Loved it. Got to talk with fascinating people who had seen the world. Was going to go to Tufts. And then …"

His gaze shadowed, and he took in another mouthful of his ice cream.

Jason's voice was gentle. "And then …?"

Xander didn't look up. "Life changes. And then I didn't go."

I finished licking off all of the jimmies and stared at the remaining ice cream on my cone.

The corner of Jason's mouth quirked up. "You're full, aren't you?"

I sheepishly grinned.

He put out a hand. "That's why I didn't order any," he explained. "Your eyes tend to be bigger than your stomach." He took the ice cream and licked a swirl into it.

I looked out over the pond. "We've got a nice corner of the world here. Places have a history to them. West End Creamery has been here over a century. The First Congregational Church, on Sutton Common, worships in a building built over one hundred fifty years ago."

Xander nodded, digging into his ice cream. "Yeah, I was there for the celebration. It was quite a thing. They had marching bands, pie-eating competitions, and even raffles."

I kept my voice light. "Oh? Did you win anything?"

His spoon scraped the bottom of his cup. "Yeah. A Santa."

I smiled. "Oh? Do you still have it? I love the variety that the Vaillancourts make. Yours must be a real treasure."

He shook his head, his gaze forlorn at the empty sundae cup before him. "I don't have it any more. I gave it to –"

His eyes sharpened, and he looked up at me. "I never said it was a Vaillancourt Santa."

I shrugged. "I just assumed that –"

He shook his head, looking more carefully between the two of us. "I should have known you two were up to something.

Offering to buy me food. Asking about me." He pushed himself to his feet. "You stay away from me!"

Jason carefully stood, easing between Xander and me. "We just wanted to know –"

Xander backed up, his face reddening. "Stay away!"

He turned and strode to his car, climbing in and slamming the door. He pulled sharply out of his space. His tires squealed as he steamed onto Purgatory Road, nearly hitting a green pick-up truck. He raced beneath the 146 overpass.

A siren squealed, and a Sutton police cruiser coming off the highway off-ramp launched after him in pursuit.

Jason looked over at me. "That could have gone better."

I sighed. "I'm sorry. I should have remembered not to mention Vaillancourt."

He shook his head. "The moment we got into that topic area he was antsy." His gazed up Purgatory Road. "He did say he gave the Santa to someone. So the question is, who?"

We sat back down, and I stared at the pond while Jason finished his ice cream. He was just tucking the last bit of cone in his mouth when his phone rang.

"Jason here."

He listened for a moment, then nodded. "Yes, that was us. Need us to come down and make a statement?" Some more listening, and he nodded again. "All right. Just let me know if you need anything."

He turned to me. "They're booking him on reckless driving, resisting arrest, and operating under the influence. Guess he must have been drinking before he got here – he blew a 0.1%."

I raised an eyebrow. "He didn't seem drunk to me."

He shrugged. "Guess he holds it well. Apparently he got feisty with the arresting officer. It seems Xander is well known by the town police, and they're expecting he'll be sitting behind those orange bars of the holding cell until tomorrow at least."

I smiled. "At least he'll get some Tony's Pizza for dinner, from what I hear."

He grinned. "Oh? Is that a request?"

"I certainly wouldn't mind some eggplant parm. And that salad they make is rather good, too."

He drew me up, then slid an arm around my waist. "Sure thing. But first, how about a walk around Purgatory Chasm, to help this ice cream course settle?"

I nodded. "And tomorrow, after my trip to the deCordova Sculpture Park, I'll head over to the Sutton Library. If he gave that Santa to someone, maybe that's why he was so excited to win it. Maybe he knew that this special someone would love it as a present. His yearbook might give us some clues."

"You are both wise and beautiful," smiled Jason.

"And agile," I teased him. "Maybe we could go climbing some birch trees."

He raised an eyebrow. "And get them to swing down to Earth?"

My eyes gleamed. "You never know."

Chapter 7

I stared at the object in front of me. It was a suit of armor, but child sized, and it was slumped against an oak tree as if its wearer had suffered a mortal blow. My hand rested on the camera hanging at my side, but I was caught by the vision. For a moment I could not bring myself to draw my eyes away.

Finally I turned to Tanya. "What do you think it is supposed to mean?"

She looked equally touched, and she gazed around the quiet woods at the other four similar sculptures. "The artist, Laura Ford, is from Wales. She's making a statement about how we send young people off to war. The innocents end up mangled."

I nodded. Mangled was certainly the word to use. The bronze figures' limbs were bent at unnatural angles, and in some cases they almost seemed to sink down into the earth.

I looked behind us. Tanya's teenaged son, Conor, was accompanying us for our exploration of the deCordova Sculpture Park for the day. Jason was off patrolling Sutton Woods, and I'd been emailing him photos of my favorite sculptures. The skies were blue, and so far we'd encountered some fascinating works of art. But this had been the first one that touched me.

I waved to Conor. "Conor, would you be in this photo for me? Pretend that the armor is Boromir, and you're Aragorn, holding him as he passes away."

For some reason, the sight of that small, damaged body upset me. It seemed to help if, even just in my viewfinder, I could give it a proper send off.

Conor smiled and dutifully moved to his position, kneeling beside the crumpled form. I had brought Jason's Canon EOS-40D with me, and I composed the shot, taking a few images.

The sight of Conor carefully cradling the small sculpture gave me a small measure of ease.

We walked along the quiet paths, and Conor moved ahead of us, texting on his phone. Tanya turned to me. "So, no identification yet on that young girl you found? That must be quite hard on you. Have the police made any progress?"

I gave a soft shrug. "We have the time frame narrowed down to perhaps ten years. You would think it would be easy, now, to know who the girl might be. But it is amazing the vast space between the enormous number of children who leave home and the few listed in missing children databases. The rest simply vanish from view." I glanced over at one of the bronze figures, the twisted form huddled beside a rock. "It's like one of these sculptures. When the artist comes and removes it, it will be as if it never existed."

Tanya shook her head, patting her camera. "We will have a record of them," she pointed out. "Surely some sort of record exists for this girl – one that did not require the parents to be responsible and fill out forms?"

I sighed. "I'll be swinging by the Sutton Library later, to check their school yearbooks. I have to start somewhere. If I'm very lucky, there'll be a local girl who is there one year and not there the next. Then it's a matter of figuring out if she went somewhere else – or simply vanished."

Tanya watched her son as he walked ahead. "Conor is nearly sixteen – and that's currently the age for dropping out in Massachusetts. It's scary to think that he and his friends could simply choose to stop going to school, and that would be the end of it. This girl could have been in the same situation. She might have decided, for whatever reason, that she was giving up on education. And then one wrong turn, into alcohol, or drugs, or prostitution, and it was all over."

I looked down. "I remember being sixteen. I thought I knew it all. I was so sure that I could handle my own life. It's only years later that I realized just how dangerous some of my choices had been."

Tanya glanced over. "And this Xander refuses to help?"

I nodded. "He refuses to speak one word of anything to anyone. Apparently the DA's office can at least hold him for now on the other charges. However, if he's not going to speak voluntarily, we can't get much help in figuring out his role in whatever went on in 1984. We'll just have to keep at it ourselves."

We approached a pair of giant heart-shaped sculptures, about ten feet tall. From a distance they seemed welcoming, almost romantic. But as we drew closer I could see they were embedded with grasping hands, twisted faces, hammers, pipes, and a myriad of other objects.

Tanya waved to Conor, then turned to me. "Would you take a photo of us by them?"

I nodded and smiled. "Of course!"

They posed before the tool-filled hearts, and I thought about the symbolism as I framed the shot, adjusting the exposure for the bright afternoon light. To me the sculptures were full of danger, almost hostility, with the pipes and metal objects embedded into them. To Tanya and Conor they were a pair of warm symbols, something representing their affection for each other. And apparently to artist Jim Dine the hearts were a quite personal statement. His grandparents had owned a hardware store, and the images were ones which brought fond memories to mind.

I took the photos, musing over the various viewpoints. One sculpture, but so many different emotions being drawn from it, all depending on how one looked at the issue.

It seemed all too soon before we returned to Tanya's house and I climbed into my Forester to head toward Sutton. A press of an icon and Jason was picking up the phone.

I could hear the smile in his voice. "How was the sculpture park?"

"Fascinating. Any news?"

"Well, apparently someone disturbed the crime scene. Dug up all around where the body had been found. The police can't figure out if the person was looking for something or just trying to muddy the waters."

I frowned. "Is Xander still in the holding cell?"

"Nope, he paid his bail. Apparently he doesn't have much of an alibi for the time the site was disturbed, either. But the police can't prove it was him."

"Well, I'm pulling into the library now, so I'll chat with you when I get home."

"Sure thing, see you soon."

The parking lot at the library was half full. I waved to the librarian at the desk before heading into the back room where the yearbooks were stored.

I pulled out the yearbooks for 1981, 1982, 1983, and 1984, and laid them one above the other on the long table. I began with the freshmen in 1981 and compared the girls with the sophomores from 1982, the juniors from 1983, and the seniors from 1984. I had reached the Ds before I found my first missing girl. Judi Doherty. I kept at it, page by page, and then worked on the other classes as well. By the end there were five missing girls. In addition to Judi, there was Michelle Hough, Cara Malden, Suzanne Russo, and Tina Walker.

I looked at the names of the five girls. Could one of those be the girl I had found at the drive-in? Each one looked happy in her carefully posed photo. What had happened to them since that snapshot in time?

I went back through the 1984 yearbook to find Xander. There he was, his hair clean-cut, his button-down shirt neatly pressed, with a gaze that said he was preparing to achieve great things. I wondered just what the hurdle was that he had met.

I moved a couple of pages ahead to the prom photos. The children seemed blissfully happy, girls and guys alike in feathered hair and bright smiles. Apparently their theme song had been "Time After Time" by Cyndi Lauper.

I could still remember the music video for the song, the young girl caught between the boy she loved and the desire to seek out her dreams. In the end the boy had to let her go – she had to take on her quest alone. The video never made clear why the boy held back, but maybe that vagueness was best. It let the watcher put in their own personal situations, the ones many of us have faced. There were so many forces that pulled young couples in different directions.

I turned another page, then stopped in surprise.

Xander was there, posing with his arm around a young woman with large, doe-brown eyes. She had long, straight brown hair which fell to her waist, quite different from the page after page of feathered shoulder-length hair I'd seen in the books. She also had a raisin-sized birthmark high on her right cheek. Where the other girls looked as if they wore Easter versions of civil war ball gowns, this young woman wore a slender, elegant, midnight-blue dress out of a 1930s movie. Her beauty was not showy and hair-band style, but more a timeless glow.

I took a photo of the page with my cellphone, then zoomed it in so my camera screen showed just the girl's face. I put the camera's image on the table as my guide. Then I went back, page by page, through each of the school yearbooks.

I could not find the girl anywhere.

I emailed the photo to Jason, then hit his icon on the main screen. He picked up on the second ring.

His voice was warm. "Hey there. Still at the library?"

"Check your email," I responded. "I think I may have found something."

There was a pause, and when he spoke again his voice held curiosity. "Where did you find this?"

"In the 1984 yearbook, from Xander's senior prom. She seems to be the right age in the photo, but I can't find her in any of the yearbooks. Maybe she's from a different school system?"

"I suppose, but which one? Do we go town by town, working out way outward, and hoping we find her? Heck, what if she was homeschooled?"

I looked down at the image. "Still, it is a start," I pointed out. "Could you forward that along to the police? Maybe they can convince him to start talking and at least tell us who this girl was. Maybe the school has some sort of record from the prom."

"Will do," he agreed. "And in the meantime, come on home to me. I miss you."

"Hold on a moment."

I took a last look at the young couple in the photo. They looked so happy, so content to be by each other's side. What had happened to them?

I closed the book, then returned the yearbooks to their shelves. I turned and spoke into the phone.

"I miss you too. Maybe we could sit by the fire pit for a while tonight?"

I could hear the smile in his voice. "I'll get the chocolate and graham crackers ready."

Chapter 8

I breathed in the freshness of the afternoon, walking along the quiet trail of Charley's Loop in Purgatory Chasm. The sunlight dappled the trail ahead, and I occasionally swung the camera off my shoulder to take a photo of a patch of moss or an oddly shaped rock. Jason was giving a presentation at an elementary school, and I didn't mind walking the trail alone. I had done so for so many years that it felt like second nature. The woods were meditative, restful, drawing my mind inward.

My doctor's appointment earlier in the afternoon had gone smoothly, no issues at all. My doctor assured me that the tiny red specks which were appearing with more frequency on my legs were apparently *cherry angiomas* and were quite common in people as they age. I also had more *Seborrheic keratosis* – another ailment of encroaching maturity. These small, scaly spots, slightly raised from the skin, made me feel as if I were turning into a lizardy Dalmatian.

When I asked my doctor if there was any treatment, she replied no – that the spots and scales were benign, and people simply lived with them. They formed crimson tattoos and clinging barnacles on our vessel in life. When I asked what caused them, I was told that doctors really didn't know.

Me being me, this meant that the moment I got home I had delved into Google. My theory of life is that a body is fairly complex and usually does things for a reason. If my body was making tiny red dots, it was probably reacting to something. Sure, I didn't expect that my right thigh's "W" of Cassiopeia meant I was soon going to be tied to a chair. But undoubtedly these crimson pinpoints were being spawned by a reaction.

To what?

Sure enough, it seemed that a number of people felt cherry angiomas were connected with too much bromide in the system – which then related to a lack of iodine. I examined the multivitamins I had recently switched to, when my store had run out of my normal Centrum Chewables. Hmmm - the new option had no iodine in them! Apparently for the past two months I'd been without my normal iodine intake – and these crimson constellations had been appearing.

Time to trust my body.

On the *Seborrheic keratosis* side, I found that skin that had been stressed was more likely to develop them. I'd had several serious bouts of poison ivy over the past few years, right where the spots were developing. Coincidence? Perhaps it was time to take better care of my skin, with Epson salt baths and a loofa, to see how my body reacted to that.

A small red squirrel scurried across my path, and I smiled. I used to think of red squirrels as endangered little creatures, being driven out by the larger grey squirrel. But Jason had reassured me that the red squirrel was doing quite fine, and if I happened to see mostly grey squirrels in my own neighborhood, this was nothing to worry about.

I reached the crossroads at the bottom of the main chasm and pulled out my phone. I sent Jason a text.

At far end. Heading back around other side of Charley's Loop.

A few moments later my phone chirped and his response came.

On break. Police still having no luck tracing girl in photo. School has no record.

I pondered my options as I began the ascent up the other side of the trail. Xander seemed unwilling to help us for whatever reason, and apparently both of his parents had passed away. We couldn't just go yearbook by yearbook through every town in New England.

I was climbing over a large, grey rock when an idea struck me. Xander might not be willing to talk – but surely he had friends in high school who had gone to the prom with him. One of them might remember the girl. It was still a long shot that the skeleton was even her, of course, but it was the only thread I had a solid hold on. I was determined to keep tugging.

When I came out of Purgatory I hopped in my car and headed over to the library. The yearbooks were waiting for me right where I had left them, and I settled down with the 1984 one. I flipped through to the prom pictures and studied them, looking to see if Xander and his date were ever photographed with any other students.

No luck. While there were other groups shown, the only time Xander showed up was in that one photo.

I continued to move forward through the pages, to the back, where the sports images were.

The Golf Team.

There Xander was, smiling, his club in hand, and his arm was draped around the shoulders of a boy about his height.

Derrick Morton, the team captain.

I pulled out my phone and did a search on "Derrick Morton Golf".

Up popped a link to Blackstone National's Friday night league.

My heart sang. Not only was Derrick still local, but he was going to be in a known place at a known time! All I had to do was go to Blackstone tomorrow night and Derrick would come to me.

My phone chirped.

Heading home. Will you be there?

I smiled.

Yes.

Chapter 9

The rain had eased by the time we pulled into the Blackstone National Golf Club parking lot, but apparently it had done its work on the day. The parking lot was all but empty. My shoulders slumped, and I looked over at Jason.

"Guess they cancelled the league play for the day," I sighed. "What do you want to do?"

He smiled. "I'm having dinner with the woman I love. That's good enough for me."

I gave his hand a squeeze, and we headed across the parking lot. The sun was poking through the clouds, sending a glimmer across the wet patio furniture, and I saw motion on one of the tables. An elegantly thin walking stick was carefully stepping across the top, first one leg, then another, its antennae sweeping in attentive watchfulness.

"Look at that!" I cried, stepping forward in delight.

Jason put out his hand. The walking stick hesitated for a moment, then deliberately walked his way up Jason's arm.

I pulled out my phone and took a few photos. "What a cool creature."

The walking stick was now perched on Jason's shoulder like a stick-figure parrot for a kayaking captain. I gently scooped it up in my hands and put it into the side grass, where it ambled off.

Jason moved to the door and held it open for me. "Shall we?"

The TV was blaring some Discovery channel show, but other than that the room was deserted. We walked over to the bar, finding the three waitresses chatting with three young men who seemed to be staff. A lone customer sat at the bar, staring up at the TV.

One of the waitresses, a slim woman with a dark ponytail, looked up with a smile. "Table for two? Would you like the bar or main restaurant area?"

Jason nudged his head back toward the larger room. "The main area, and could we mute the TV?"

"We can turn it off!" she responded brightly. In a moment we were settled by the large windows overlooking the course.

We glanced over the menu, and by the time the waitress had come over we were ready. Jason ordered the steak, while I asked for the chicken, with veggies rather than pasta, and a side salad. Red wine for him, white for me. She nodded and was off to put in the order.

I looked around the room. "Guess they won't be having the live music tonight."

He patted my hand. "I'll play you some songs when we get home."

I smiled. "I would like that."

A blond man in a neon-orange polo shirt and khaki shorts strolled out of the restrooms, calling into the bar area. "See ya all tomorrow. I'm heading home." There was a chorus of farewells in response.

I looked at him in surprise. "Derrick Morton?"

He had aged gracefully – his face was nearly identical to his high school self, and just a few lines showed where life had worn him in. He gazed at me in curiosity. "That's me. I'm sorry, do I know you?"

I stood, putting out a hand. "Morgan Warren, and this is my boyfriend, Jason Rowland. I was doing some research on your high school class, and I came across your photo on the golf team."

He grinned widely and came over to plunk down at the seat next to me. "Ah, those high school years. Those were some of the best years of my life! The golf team, the girls, the long, lazy summers."

The waitress came over with my salad and looked down to Derrick. "Another beer?"

Derrick glanced at Jason. "I wouldn't want to intrude …"

"Not at all," replied Jason with a smile. He looked up to the waitress. "Put it on our bill."

Derrick nodded his thanks, then leant back in his chair. "Ah, I remember the days. I'd do eighteen rounds in the morning, scarf down a sandwich and a Coke, then go out for another eighteen in the afternoon."

The waitress brought back his beer, and he drank down a sip. "So, what is it you wanted to know? I set a number of records during my years at Sutton High, and several of them still stand."

I looked over at the fieldstone fireplace, currently unlit. "I think Blackstone was built in 1999, right?"

He nodded. "It wasn't around when I was growing up, and Pleasant Valley was too pricey for us. Heck, even Clearview in Millbury only got put up a few years after I graduated. But I had a friend over at Green Hill, in Worcester, so I got to play there. Nice course."

"Do you stay in touch with Xander?"

He laughed, the corners of his eyes crinkling. "Xander? I doubt he knows which end of a club to hold any more. I think he gathers up excess books from libraries and sells them on eBay, or something like that." He took a drink. "He's a long way from his golden boy days."

I glanced at Jason, raising an eyebrow, before turning back to Derrick. "Oh? What happened?"

He leant forward, his brow furrowing. His voice snapped with heat. "It was all that bitch's fault," he growled. "She ripped his heart out of him. She might have looked like a sculpture come to life, but her innards were coal black." The corner of his mouth quirked. "Glad I didn't end up with her, after all. She was toxic."

"Oh? What was her name?"

"Mary," he replied without hesitation. "Mary Goldstein. Lived out in Worcester." Derrick shook his head. "Xander thought he had it made. The girl, college, his whole life mapped out in front of him. And then, poof, it was gone. She took off on him and he lost his will." He waved his hand in the air. "And look at him now."

The waitress brought over the two plates of food, and Derrick downed the rest of his beer. "Well, I'll let you folks eat in peace. Thanks for the beer; it was nice talking with you."

I shook his hand. "Thank you for your time."

He gave a wave, then sauntered out through the glass doors.

I looked at Jason. "Mary Goldstein from Worcester. So that was why we didn't find her in the Sutton records. But if she's the girl we found in the drive-in, why didn't anybody report her missing?"

He shrugged, taking a bite of his steak. "If it is her, I guess we'll find out when we see if she has family around."

There was a movement from the bar area, and I looked up. A smile brightened my face. "Charles! I didn't know you were here."

Charles was a retired banker we had met last November, and he occasionally ran into us when we ate here at the Blackstone National Golf Course. He was bumbling but friendly. I had helped him mend a rift that had developed back in the Age of Aquarius, involving the lawyer we'd seen a few days ago over at Pleasant Valley.

I waved at the seat that Derrick had just vacated. "Come, join us."

He walked over and put his drink in front of him, nodding to Jason. "So you two were enjoying the tales of Derrick the Dashing?"

My brows raised with interest. "Not a fan?"

He shrugged. "The boy's just a little too full of himself for my tastes," he returned. "He was a golf hero back in the 80s, and he thinks it will carry him through life." He gave a snort. "Acting all sad about the Mary situation, when it's the best thing that could ever have happened to him."

My interest perked up. "Oh? Why is that?"

He glanced out at the deepening sunset. "Word has it that his friend, Xander, was a far better golfer than Derrick. Derrick had the flash and the charm, but Xander was the real deal. When it came time for scholarships, both boys had their eye set on Tufts and wanted the school's golf scholarship. Derrick was

convinced he'd be a shoo-in, after schmoozing various members
of the faculty. But then the announcement came – and Xander
got it." Charles rolled his eyes. "Derrick was insufferable."

"You knew him back then?"

He nodded. "I played at Green Hill in those days, and he was
always hanging around there."

"So then what happened?"

He took a drink. "Just like Derrick said. Mary took off on
Xander, and the lad was devastated. He adored her. He was laid
low by the blow and never sent in any of the paperwork for
Tufts. He defaulted on his scholarship, on everything. And it
went to Derrick instead."

I glanced at Jason. "Sounds like it worked out great for
Derrick."

Charles nodded. "It did indeed. He made the best of those
four years. Ended up doing quite well for himself."

He shrugged. "In any case, just thought you might want to
know that there was more to the story than he was telling." He
finished off his drink and stood. "Got to get home, but nice
seeing you."

"Sure thing, you too," I responded, and he was out the door.

I turned to Jason. "What do you think?"

He glanced at his watch. "Well, it's clearly after hours on a
Friday night, and I hate to get the police off on a wild goose
chase when we should be able to easily figure out if she's still
alive or not. We don't even know if she's really related to the
case or not. I suggest we look into it over the weekend, and if
we can't find her at all by Monday morning, we send the news
along. What do you think?"

I nodded. "Sounds like a reasonable compromise to me."

The waitress came by. "Ready to wrap those up?"

I nodded. "And I think one brownie sundae, with two
spoons."

Jason's eyes gleamed, and he reached over to take my hand.
"You know, if we have chocolate this late in the evening, you're
not likely to be sleepy for quite some time."

My grin filled my face.

"Exactly."

Chapter 10

Jason was off doing a patrol of the Rutland State Park, Juliet was curled up at my feet in a purring sphere, and I was reading an article from the Worcester Telegram on my PC. The article was from April 1984, and its feature was Mary Goldstein. She'd been a sophomore in high school. Tall, elegant, her dark eyes had soulfulness which the photo seemed to capture well.

Mary had been a watercolor painter. No, that put it too mildly. That made it sound like she took a little plastic pack of colors, the kind elementary school kids adored, and went down to the Blackstone River for a Saturday to plunk down cerulean and lime colored splotches which generally approximated a rush of water past a bank.

No. Even at that young age, Mary was a talented artist.

More than that, Mary had a vision. Her chosen field of interest was the victims of the Holocaust.

Mary's own parents had been tragically taken from her when she was thirteen, in a drunk-driver car crash. Her two older brothers, her seniors by ten and twelve years, both promptly moved home to take care of her. Her parents had been camera-shy, and Mary was upset by the lack of photos remaining of the two. Then, studying World War II in a history class, she realized that the trauma she faced was nothing compared with those whose family members went into the gates of Auschwitz, Treblinka, and the other extermination camps. The horror of it wore at her and she sought for a way to help.

Her path was through her art.

She would meet with the family and learn everything she could about the person she was to paint. What was known of their features, what they liked, what their hopes and dreams were. She took photos of living relatives to get a sense of the family bone structure and skin tone.

And then she painted.

The Telegram article featured several of her paintings. I was deeply touched by the way Mary had brought the people to life. For many of these families, this image was all they had to remember the person they had lost. I could imagine one of the paintings hanging over a family's fireplace, or holding a place of honor in a dining room. Mary was truly helping these families heal.

Mary had received a great deal of support from Temple Emanuel, which she attended. Another Google browse quickly helped me discover that just two months ago Temple Emanuel had merged with Temple Sinai, becoming, logically, Temple Emanuel Sinai.

In the article Mary gave thanks to her two brothers, her faith, and to her school mentor who had helped encourage her in her path. "The world should never forget," Mary was quoted as saying, "and with my small actions, I hope to help the families remember."

I was touched by the article and by the immense talent of the young woman. I returned to Google to see what else Mary had done after the article's date.

Nothing.

I tried a variety of word combinations, but there was no luck. There simply was no record of Mary having done anything of note after that April article.

I shook my head. Had she abandoned her project and faded into obscurity? Or was this a sign that she really could be the girl we sought?

I looked up the website for Temple Emanuel Sinai and found contact information. I sent off an email, asking if I could come in to talk with someone about Mary Goldstein and her works.

The phone rang, and I picked it up. I gave my voice a soft lilt. "Hey there, sweetie."

Jason chuckled. "What did people do before caller ID?"

"I would have known anyway," I teased him. "Nobody else calls the house phone. Well, nobody but the occasional telemarketers. And I bet sweetie would be the best thing they've been called all week."

I could hear the smile on his face. "Probably true. One hour warning, I'll pick you up at 6:30 p.m. for tonight's benefit gig."

"I'll be ready!"

I had plenty of time to go through my shower, brush out my hair, and don my custom-made t-shirt for the evening. A few weeks ago I'd had some fun with fabric paints and a $3.99 dark blue shirt from Michael's, creating a band logo shirt complete with palm trees. Jason had even added on some gold edging with a metallic sharpie. The end result was quite nice, if I had to say so myself. Certainly nothing when compared with Mary's haunting images, but I had to start somewhere.

I heard Jason's car in the driveway, and I gathered up my cameras and purse before heading out to meet him. He gave me a kiss on the cheek, waiting for me to buckle in before he backed out again. "How was your day?"

I filled him in on my research as we drove. "If she really is the girl we found," I ended, "it would be a great shame. She was making a difference for a large number of people. I think she would have gone even further had she been given the chance."

Jason's eyes shadowed. "It does seem odd that a girl with so much talent, receiving such recognition for her good causes, could simply vanish from all record. Surely there should be notes about her earning scholarships to art school, or working with famous organizations, or *something*."

My phone chirped, and I looked down. "Ah, here we go. The rabbi at Temple Emmanuel Sinai says he's available to meet me Sunday, any time. Apparently Mary was an important person in their congregation, and he's happy to discuss her works."

Jason nodded. "That's a good sign. We had planned to go down to my reunion with my high school friends, after the benefit, but if you'd rather –"

I smiled at him. "I'd rather go with you, of course," I interrupted. "We were planning to be back home on Sunday by six, yes? Let me see if the rabbi would be open to an evening meeting, perhaps at his home."

I sent off the email. A few minutes later I received a response.

Certainly, 7 p.m. would be fine. I look forward to talking with you then.

"There we go," I informed Jason. "Everything will work out just right."

He smiled at that. "It always does, in the end."

We turned into the Millbury VFW post. They had undergone renovations in recent years, and now a Fidelity Bank fronted the building. There were a number of motorcycles in the parking lot, undoubtedly from the bike run which had come at the beginning of the benefit. We drove around to the back side, and Jason began unloading his gear. The singer and drummer were already there, arranging their gear in the side preparation room.

Meredith put out her arms to me. "Thank you so much for coming, Morgan! This is such a good cause."

I returned her hug. "Cancer is such an insidious disease," I mused. "It can strike any of us, and it is scary that doctors still think a reasonable solution is to bombard the entire body with chemicals or radiation. In fifty years they will look back on us as living in the dark ages."

She nodded. "Well, I was just reading that they think the days of chemotherapy may be coming to an end. They have developed enough customized protocols that they can better target just the cancer cells, without having to flood the entire body with toxins."

The microphone suddenly sprang into life from the main room, and a male voice launched into a song at a volume which shook my eardrums. I glanced at Meredith, then walked to step into the main hall. The stage, to the left, held a traditional foursome of guitarist, bassist, singer, and drummer. To the right there were eight large, round tables set up, all filled with people, and then many more patrons standing along the bar to the back.

My ears shuddered like a jackhammer with the volume.

I moved back into the side room, and Jason came in from outside, carrying his guitar case. He looked at the hall in surprise as a guitar solo sliced through the room. "Is the sound man really setting the volume that high?"

Meredith shook her head. "Apparently the band is overriding the sound man," she explained. "They want it loud."

Jason glanced at me. "At this volume, I'll lose my hearing before we go on. Care for a walk outside?"

I instantly nodded my head, and the drummer joined us as we strolled around the parking lot. The music was still clearly audible there, and I wondered just what kind of hearing loss those inside were suffering.

* * *

The benefit was a success, and we were driving south on 495 to Jason's friend in Easton. Jason's voice held a smile. "Apparently they were up until 4 a.m. last night, tasting whiskies," he explained. "They get together every year, and everyone sprawls on air mattresses and couches."

"We could have brought our tent, if you wanted," I mused.

He shook his head. "We'll get there after midnight as it is, and it's just the one night." He glanced over. "Unless you mind sharing the air mattress in the game room?"

I smiled. "Not at all."

When we rolled up to the large colonial, the house was dark. We carefully crept in through the front door; there were snores and murmurs from all around us. We found Jason's friend, Patrick, still awake in the kitchen, waiting for us. He looked up, rueful. "Guess we wore ourselves out last night," he joked.

"That means more time to talk tomorrow," smiled Jason.

Patrick nudged his head to the back porch. "Still, we can watch for meteors. They should be right over the back yard."

We went out, and right as we stepped onto the porch a large meteor streaked down and left before flaring into the blackness.

I gave Jason a hug. "Perfect timing!"

Chapter 11

There was a gentle knocking on the door, and a tall, smiling woman with reddish hair poked her head into the room. "I'm sorry to wake you, but it's ten-thirty and the kids will want access to their games soon," she explained. "I do have eggs and bacon ready for you, though!"

Jason waved with a sleepy hand, and in a moment he'd climbed up from the air mattress. I joined him a bit more slowly. Whether it was the departure from my usual night-hours routine, the strange location, or just the high from the gig last night, I hadn't managed to sleep a wink. I wondered how long I'd last before my energy faded.

For now, though, I ran my hands through my hair and helped Jason drain the air from the mattress. Then we stepped through the living room and into the kitchen, where apparently the entire household of guests was congregating. One by one I was introduced to his old friends, their wives, and a plethora of exceedingly energetic children. The names vanished from my mind as quickly as they were presented, but I sensed they wouldn't mind.

The tall woman looked at me with a grin. "And I'm Joanne. Come, sit by me so we can chat. What will you have to eat?"

Jason had poured my protein shake into a glass and handed it over. "This is it."

Joanne arched an eyebrow. "Are you sure? I can make you something, it's no problem."

I shook my head. "I'm just not in the mood to eat when I first wake up," I explained. "So this gets me protein and vitamins, and tides me over until I actually get hungry."

"Fair enough," she agreed.

Patrick sat down at her left. "We saw all sorts of meteors last night, after you sleepyheads went to bed."

She glanced around her. "You try feeding this horde, and you'll get worn out fairly quickly too!"

The children finished up with their muffins and cereal and in a moment were racing into the back yard. I heard splashes and cries of delight as they launched themselves into the pool.

Patrick looked over to me. "So, Jason says you run websites?"

I nodded and explained to him about the different sites I maintained. Patrick and Joanne drew me along into the conversation, and I found myself relaxing. By the time breakfast had finished, I felt as if I'd known the couple for a long while.

Patrick looked up to Jason. "Well, shall we?"

Jason glanced over to me. I smiled and nodded. "Go have your fun."

The men trooped out to a table set up in a shady nook of the back yard. One of the wives smiled, watching them go. "They've been playing that same role-playing campaign for over ten years now. Every year we get together for the weekend, and every year they pick up right where they left off."

She snagged a book off the table. "And now I'm going to catch up on some reading."

The kitchen seemed church-quiet after the near chaos of a short while earlier. I stood to gather up the plates and cups while Joanne emptied the previous batch of dishes and loaded in the fresh set. She looked out the back window as she worked, shaking her head with a smile. "There Jason goes, running his hand through his hair. He's been doing that since high school. I swear, their hair greys, and they grow a paunch, but they're the same boys they've always been."

I found her disinfecting wipes and began wiping down the table. "So you've known them all since high school?"

She nodded. "They were all smart, even back then. And look at them now. One's a surgeon, one's at NASA, one's an English professor. Patrick handles computer systems."

A grin quirked my mouth. "And Jason is a forest ranger."

She chuckled. "I'm sure you know as well as I do that Jason is brilliant. The ranger system is blessed to have him. He has a way of communicating with everyone he meets, from the roughest hunters to the youngest children, that leaves them feeling respected and enriched." She slid the last plate into the dishwasher and latched it closed. A push of a button, and a soft, watery murmur began. "He always says that he gets back the energy he puts out. It's why he's never had any sort of altercation, in the nearly twenty long years he's been rangering."

I nodded. "I used to think that a ranger was sort of a police officer in a forest setting, there to catch poachers and bring in vagrants. But I've learned since then that it's more being a guardian of the forest, as well as an educator to the people who use it."

One of the wives came in from the living room, shepherding along a pair of young girls. "The lemonade is out on the back porch," she told them. "Go play!"

She sat down to join us, glancing around to ensure no youngsters were within hearing. She dropped her voice down a notch. "So, tell us about this situation you and Jason are looking into."

By the time I finished describing the story, and answered all their various questions, lunchtime had wrapped around. I ladled the potato salad and macaroni salad into serving containers, Patrick set up trays of burgers and hot dogs, and Joanne put out piles of condiments. Then the troops were called in.

The end of the meal seemed to signal the end of the gathering. Families looked for lost pink crocs and missing backpacks. I stood in the front door hallway with the others, beneath the large certificate from the Pope blessing Patrick and Joanne's wedding back in 1989.

Patrick was shaking one of the men's hands. "And we should get out to Higgins Armory before they close down," Patrick advised the man. "Only a few months left before December."

The man, slender and dark haired, shook his head. "I can't believe that SCA members didn't rally to save it. Higgins must not have let them know. Higgins was reputed to have the largest collection of medieval armor and weaponry in the western hemisphere. And now most will go into the cellars of the Worcester Art Museum."

I shook my head. "Most SCA members I know don't have a lot of spare money," I pointed out. "They're just not interested."

"I know some SCA members with money," he countered. "There should have been some way to save it."

I nodded, keeping quiet. I lived only fifteen minutes from Higgins and was well aware of its plight – as was probably every historian within a three hour radius. The SCA members definitely knew about Higgins's impending demise – but by and large that ranked far lower on their list of things to worry about than other, pressing needs. The proof was in the results. Despite everything that had been tried for the past three years, Higgins was closing its doors.

At last Joanne and Patrick turned to Jason and me. Patrick clasped Jason in a hug. "It was good to see you, as always. Maybe we can get together sometime soon, just the four of us."

Jason nodded. "I would like that."

We all exchanged hugs, and then we climbed into the car and headed back up north.

Jason looked over. "A bit overwhelming, with everyone all at once, I know."

I smiled reassuringly. "They were friendly and welcoming," I assured him. The corner of my mouth tweaked up. "Although I did find one aspect of it intriguing."

His eyebrow went up. "Oh?"

I leant back in my seat. "Just last week I was helping a new writer with his science fiction story. He had it set in the far future. In one scene the men were out playing basketball in the back yard while the wives were inside washing dishes. I told him that those types of sixties gender roles were long gone. That we didn't even have that happen in our present, never mind in a far-off future. He agreed and altered the scene."

I chuckled. "And then, here we have a group of well-educated men and women, and the men all go off to play a game all afternoon. Meanwhile the women are wiping down the counters, filling the dishwasher, and preparing the condiments."

"I thought I saw Patrick go in?"

I nodded. "Yes, he did come to help out with the burgers and hot dogs. Maybe that is stereotypical too, that the men do the meat and grilling tasks, while the women handle the washing." I watched the trees on the highway's banks stream by in a wave of dark green. "But you note that the English professor, or the NASA scientist, didn't come in to put food back into the fridge. It was a wife who sat by my side and helped put the salads back into their containers."

He nodded. "I suppose that's true."

"And then there's all the children in the house, and they're watching this," I mused. "What are they learning, about how men and women interact? What kind of lessons do they absorb about who should do what? Maybe that men are called when something heavy needs to be lifted. But that women will sit there and wash dishes and clean counters while the guys laugh and drink."

I grinned. "I told Joanne how you do all the cooking at home, and it was as if she couldn't believe it. She couldn't fathom that there could be a version of the world where a man did the cooking and a woman simply enjoyed the results."

His eyes twinkled. "She hasn't tasted your cooking."

I nodded. "And hopefully never will," I agreed.

We chatted the rest of the ride home, and by the time we arrived it was nearly six. I took a quick shower, gathered up a notebook, then gave Jason a kiss before heading north into Worcester.

Rabbi Schmidt had a small but well-maintained house in an affluent neighborhood of Worcester. I pulled up before it just at the stroke of seven. I walked up the granite stone path to the front steps and gave a gentle knock on the door.

The man who pulled open the door was in his mid-forties, with short, brown hair and kind eyes. He was slightly taller than me, and sported a healthy build, like a soccer player who has aged gracefully. He put out a hand. "Welcome to my home. I am Rabbi Schmidt."

"Morgan Warren. Thank you so much for seeing me on such short notice."

He nodded, stepping back and drawing me in. "You said it involved Mary Goldstein. Her work is treasured in our congregation. Anything I can do to share information on her efforts, I will gladly spend time on."

We moved into his living room, a comfortable combination of burgundy upholstered couches and family photos along the fireplace's mantle. Hanging over the mantle was a gorgeous watercolor of a river curling its way down to a large waterfall. The sides of the riverbanks were ablaze in golden forsythia, and a gently sloping hill on the right held a scattering of violets.

I looked at the print, at the serenity flowing from the scene. "This is the Blackstone River, at the falls in Sutton," I murmured. "It's lovely."

He nodded. "Now you see why we treasure Mary so much. She had a gift given by God."

I drew in a breath, then settled onto one of the couches. He brought over a bulbous glass water pitcher with two glasses. "Would you rather have coffee, tea, or something else?"

"Water is fine," I let him know.

He sat down opposite me. "So, how can I help you?"

Now that I was here with the rabbi, my throat closed up. I had meant just to get background information from him, to try to sense if the body Jason and I had found could really be that of Mary Goldstein. If the rabbi could not provide information about Mary's current whereabouts, I would then turn everything over to the police for them to pursue. After all, this was still quite a longshot.

But, looking into his warm gaze, a sense of peace descended over me. He had been leading this congregation for over four years and had seen them through some tumultuous changes. I had a feeling that he would be a voice of wisdom for me in what I was doing.

"I ... I'm worried that harm may have come to Mary," I found myself saying.

His brow creased, but his face remained serene. "Why do you believe that?"

"Because I think ... I think I may have found her body in the Sutton drive-in."

His fingers twined in his lap. "I heard about that. A young woman's skeleton was found about two weeks ago. That was you who came across the poor girl?"

I nodded. "My boyfriend Jason and I were looking for something else, and we found her in a shallow grave. There was an item with her. We found the boy who had first owned the item, and he had been dating Mary at the time."

I looked up at him, and a sense of pleading grew within me. "I was hoping that you could tell me that someone in the Temple had heard from Mary, had seen her, sometime after the summer of 1984. That seems to be the timeframe that her death occurred in. If just one person has seen her since then, I can rest easy. I'll know that such a special woman is still out there somewhere."

His gaze shadowed. "I am afraid that I can offer no such consolation."

My heart thundered in my chest, and I sat back in surprise. I had geared myself up to believe this would be a casual conversation – that he would point me to where she was living now and explain my inability to find her. Maybe she had married young and taken on her married name. Maybe a tragic accident had hurt her hands, so she was unable to paint, but she became a great art teacher instead. I had not believed, deep in my heart, that the delicate ivory bones nestled in the mulch could be the final remains of such a brilliant soul.

I found my voice. "How can you be so sure, so quickly? You only joined the Temple in 2009, according to the website."

He nodded. "Yes, that is true." He glanced at the painting, and his eyes softened. "In 1982, when she was only fourteen, she won a great honor. She was awarded the best artist in Massachusetts by a state-wide panel. Note that it wasn't just the best *young* artist. She was competing against talented artists of all ages. Her winning upset many people, but you can see there that her prize was deserved. She had a gift which came from her soul." He gave a soft smile. "Even her mentor used to say that she barely had to teach Mary. She just had to point her in a direction and stand back."

My brow creased. "So how does her 1982 win relate to now?"

He took a sip of water. "One of our Temple secretaries is strongly involved in artistic projects. She wanted us to develop a thirty year anniversary show of Mary's works, in 2012. It would both celebrate Mary's skills and help ensure our younger generation remembers what Jewish people have endured." His eyes grew somber. "Some things should never be forgotten."

I nodded in agreement. "So your Temple sought out Mary?"

He templed his fingers, resting his chin on them. "We did indeed. We talked with her two brothers. We talked with her mentor. We spoke with her friends from high school and anybody else we could think of." He gave a soft shrug. "We could find no trace of her."

I ran a hand through my hair. "But she was only sixteen. Surely some notice would have been paid, if such a talented girl suddenly vanished?"

He nodded. "That is why it is still so hard to take in. See, we were all under the impression that she had won an enormous grant in Germany. We thought she had left for Germany, that summer in 1984, and was working with prestigious art institutions on momentous projects."

I shook my head. "And never heard from her? And never saw her name mentioned?"

He gave a soft smile. "She never liked the publicity. That was always her mentor stirring up the press. From what I hear, Alice could be a bit … enthusiastic about her efforts. And Mary's brothers had controlled every aspect of her life once their parents died. They drove her to and from school, sat over her while she did homework, and would not allow her to watch

TV. Her friends said she chafed in that environment, beneath her brothers' harsh attention."

He spread his hands. "Apparently those who knew her figured she saw her chance for freedom and she took it. Our consensus was that she immersed herself in her work, refused to be given credit for her creations, and finally was in an environment where her creativity could fully blossom."

He sighed. "Most of her friends were happy for her and had no desire to have her found. They figured that Alice and the brothers, once they knew where to find Mary, would fly out immediately and try to drag her home again."

He looked down into his water. "But to think … all those years …"

I drew my phone out of my purse. "I think I need to make a phone call."

He wearily nodded. "I think you do, too."

Chapter 12

I blearily blinked my eyes open. The flat display of the phone on the bedside table read 1:30 p.m. Apparently my sleep deprivation had finally caught up with me. After the police and Jason had arrived at the rabbi's home, it was nearly midnight by the time I had gotten home. I had barely made it to bed before I fell sound asleep.

I poured myself a shake, gave Juliet a rub where she lay curled up on the futon in the living room, then moved into my office. Jason was giving a talk to high school students who were interested in a job in the ranger service. I imagined, by the time he was done with them, that every one of them would be dreaming of joining up.

I sat down at my desk and clicked on the screen. And groaned.

In the few days I'd been away, my inbox had blossomed to over 1,600 messages.

I drew on a smile, put on a playlist of Enya and Clannad, and set to work.

It was just after five when Jason came home, walking over behind me to gently knead at my shoulders. "Let me guess. You haven't moved from this spot since you woke up."

I nodded, rolling my head to the left to give his fingers better access. "And my shoulders are letting me know it, too."

"We have some time before my band practice tonight. Want to take a ride into Millbury?"

I looked up at him. "Oh? What for?"

"Mary's two brothers own a plumbing business, and their office is over on Grove Street. Right near Assumption Catholic Church. I thought maybe we could go talk with them a bit, about Mary."

My brow furrowed. "Won't the police already have talked with them?"

He nodded. "They have, and the brothers apparently have a hostile relationship with law enforcement. Their rap sheet is peppered with resisting arrest and disorderly charges. So the brothers were not quite … cooperative."

I lifted an eyebrow. "You think we might do better?"

He gave a shrug. "We could at least try."

I climbed up out of my chair, rolling my shoulders. "I will certainly give it my best shot."

It was only fifteen minutes before we pulled up outside the dark, shade-drawn offices of Barry and Ephraim Goldstein. A closed sign hung in the main window. I got out of the car anyway, and Jason came up to my side as we stared at the blank white shades.

I sighed. "No hours posted, but maybe they simply took the day off. They might have been shocked by the news about their sister."

A pair of teenage girls with long, brown hair sauntered down the street, their jean shorts and cut-off white t-shirts more revealing than any swimsuit I'd ever worn. One of them winked at Jason before commenting, "Looking for the plumbers? Mario and Luigi? They're down at the Milltowne."

I looked into a pair of eyes done with neon blue eye-shadow in a style Cleopatra might have been jealous of. "Oh?"

She nodded in a knowing fashion. "It's after three. They'll be at the bar."

The other one nudged her in the ribs. "Ready to take on Bowser in Blue!"

The two burst into gales of laughter, and the first sent Jason a pouty air-kiss before they turned to continue their saunter down the street.

Jason looked at me, a twinkle in his eyes. "Shall we heed the message of the sirens?"

I gave him a swat. "Sirens, my foot. They were more like jezebels." I glanced up the street. "And right in front of a church, too. What is our world coming to?"

He chuckled, moving back to the car. "That's the same thing parents said to their kids in the sixties, when they wore their hair long and danced under the stars. And the same thing the parents said to their kids in the forties, when the wild teens were necking, unchaperoned, in dark drive-ins."

I climbed into the car with him. "We've never gone to a drive-in together."

His eyes shone. "Oh? Want to go necking with me?"

I leant over and gave him a warm kiss. I murmured in his ear, "Any time."

He grinned, putting the car into gear. "First, the brothers. Then, practice." He pulled away from the curb. "And then I take you home."

Jason's band had played the Milltowne Tavern a few months back, as a three-piece when the drummer was away on vacation. It was a low, narrow building, tucked in between residential houses and the Elm Draught House – a small movie theater that played second-run films and let you eat while you watched.

There was a couple playing pool to the right as we entered and a trio of barely-legal boys watching sports on the TV to the left. A pair of heavy men in their late fifties were at the bar, their heads bent over pints of beer, their grey t-shirts and blue jeans fairly grimy with grease and sweat.

I glanced at Jason, and we walked over to take the seats one stool away from them. The bartender came over, a slender woman of perhaps thirty with an ebony ponytail and a tight teal shirt.

Jason held up two fingers. "Two Sam Adams, please."

"Bottle or draft?"

"Draft."

The waitress nodded, and in a moment we had our pint glasses. I took a long sip of mine, fortifying myself.

The men were hostile to cops, and, judging from the stories, they had a controlling attitude toward their sister. They probably thought of her as incapable of handling life on her own. I wondered if that attitude extended to women in general. It was worth a try.

I dropped my head, looking into my glass. I kept my voice to a soft murmur, hopefully just loud enough that the brothers would hear. "I still can't believe how mean those police were to me," I sighed. "I only found the poor girl in the woods by accident. I didn't even know her. But I think they were going to keep me in that room all night long!"

Jason patted me on the hand. "You did the best you could."

I turned the glass around in its spot. "And the nightmares. I think they're getting worse. I just wish I knew something – anything – about her. I think my mind would settle. But I just keep seeing her skeleton, coming for me …"

I put my head down.

The brother closer to me spoke, his voice low and gravelly. "You are the two who found the body in the Sutton drive-in?"

I nodded my head morosely. "I'm Morgan Warren. And this is Jason Rowland. We were just looking for a friend's Airsoft gun. And the next thing I know, the police are bullying us as if we had robbed a bank."

"I'm Barry, and this is my brother Ephraim. You don't have to tell us about the police. We have had our fill of them all last night and this morning. They are vultures. Here we are the innocent family members, and they make us feel like we're the culprits."

I looked up into his bloodshot eyes, the color of shadowed pond water. "Family members?"

He nodded. "We are the brothers of the girl who is missing." He paused for a long moment, then it was as if he had to force the word through his mouth. "Mary."

"I'm so sorry."

Barry took a long drink of his beer. "She was an angel. Our mother named her for the Virgin Mary, you know. Once our parents passed, my brother and I swore we would do them proud. We watched over her night and day, as vigilant as any guardian angels."

Jason's voice was low. "If it does turn out that the girl we found was your sister, we're sorry for your loss."

He shook his head. "We lost her a long time ago," he muttered. "She was abandoning us for some high-faluting project in Germany. Mary made it clear that she would leave us behind; that we no longer mattered to her." He took a long drink on his beer. "If it's her, maybe it's better this way. At least now we have a grave to visit and can perform the rites." He gave a snort. "If she'd left, she would have been lost to us completely."

"But who would have wanted to hurt her?"

Ephraim leant over, his build thicker, more muscular. "Who *didn't* want to hurt her," he corrected with a thick growl. "That mentor of hers was always pushing Mary to paint, paint, paint, as if she were some sort of an automaton with one mission in life. The works were snatched up by galleries across the state." He shrugged. "Probably half the artists in Massachusetts were furious with Mary for achieving such great heights at such a young age. They were jealous of her."

I pitched my voice to be mildly curious. "Did she have any sort of a boyfriend?"

Ephraim's eyes darkened. "I warned her to stay away from him," he scowled. "Completely the wrong sort for her. Nothing but trouble. But you know how girls are at that age. No common sense at all. All he had to do was look into her eyes, and she turned into a puppet, willing to do whatever he asked. She didn't care what he did to her, as long as she could be his."

I glanced at Jason in concern before looking back to the brothers. "Do you think this boyfriend could have hurt her?"

Barry nodded. "Absolutely. If he thought she was going to leave him, he would have been a wild man. He would have done anything to prevent her from going."

I took a sip of my beer. "Maybe he would have gone with her."

Barry crinkled his face in disbelief. "What, and give up his college plans? Not a chance. He had his life planned out. College, job, dutiful wife."

Ephraim gave a snort. "Like that ever works out."

Barry looked over at his brother. "Your wife stayed with you for five years," he pointed out. "So it worked for a little while."

Ephraim drained his glass, and the bartender came over with a fresh one without being asked. He took a swallow of that before shaking his head at his brother. "Five years of nagging about why we couldn't afford to go on cruises, like all her friends did," he growled. "And then she left me for that pock-faced dentist."

"At least you got five years," pointed out Barry. "Estelle barely gave me the time of day, because my job wasn't fancy enough. She only wanted to talk to the investment bankers and the college professors."

"You could have moved on, found someone else to chase," pointed out his brother.

"*You* try moving on," muttered Barry, as if this was a conversation they had had many times. "And, besides, it's going to be the same no matter where we go. Women judge men by the size of their wallet. Plain and simple. Little else matters to them."

They dropped into a discontented silence.

I glanced at Jason, then finished my beer. I turned to the two men. "Thank you for talking with me; I think I feel better now that I know a bit more about her. Maybe I can sleep at night now."

Barry glanced up at Jason. "You two married?"

He shook his head. "No."

"Keep it that way," warned Barry. "Women change once they get that ring on them. They have all these notions about what a husband should or should not do. They fantasize about how they will be treated as a wife. I've seen it a thousand times." He collapsed back into silence.

"I'll keep that in mind," murmured Jason. "Good night."

He guided me out of the bar, and we climbed into his car. He looked over at me as we pulled onto the road. "Well, that was interesting."

"Do you think, if it is indeed Mary, that they could have done it?"

He gave the idea some thought. "I suppose it's possible, but she was their sister. She was their entire life, once their parents passed away. Their responsibility. It would be fairly far-fetched for them to want her dead rather than out in the world performing such meaningful work."

I nodded. "I agree. And it does seem that there are a number of people who had unhealthy relationships with the poor girl." I sighed. "Including the boyfriend. We've heard about his temper. If he took her to a drive-in, and she informed him that she was going to Europe, he could easily have melted down."

It seemed only minutes before we pulled up in front of Adam the drummer's beautiful log-cabin-style home. Massive old growth pine trees towered along the edges of his property. Meredith and Paul were already there, unloading their gear, and Adam was lending a hand with a microphone stand.

Jason smiled at me. "Why don't you get the cooler in the back. I brought us a treat, compliments of Patrick and Joanne. They sent us home with some leftovers from the weekend."

I moved to the rear of the truck and popped open the cooler. There were eight Coronas in there, as well as a couple of limes, a package of cheddar slices, and a stick of pepperoni.

In a short while we'd settled in to Adam's basement and I was leaning back in my chair, tapping my toes as I enjoyed a personalized concert. The quartet was amazingly tight, with Meredith's vocals soaring up over the guitar, bass, and drums. They went through a number of songs, from Adele's "Rolling in the Deep" to Anna Nalick's "Breathe (2 am)", from Elvis's "That's All Right, Mama" to Cee Lo Green's "Forget You."

They took a break so Adam could smoke, and Jason and Paul followed him out, discussing the treble levels on the last song. I turned to Meredith. "It seems sometimes like half the songs out there are about dysfunctional relationships."

She chuckled. "We do sing Zeppelin's 'Thank You,'" she pointed out. "And the Beatles's 'I Saw Her Standing There.'"

"Ah, but is that really love or obsession?"

She grinned. "Maybe a mixture of both."

I took a drink of my Corona. "But just look at 'Forget You.' The guy is complaining because his girl is a gold digger; all she wanted from him was cash. But then guys are quite happy to sing about women being a *Brick House*. In that Beatles song, Paul only cares that the girl looks hot. He's not worried at all about her interests or points of view."

Meredith nodded. "You're preaching to the choir. After my surgery I'm down to two-thirty, but I'm nowhere near slim. Thank God I found my husband, who loves me no matter what size I am. But for many guys, all they care about is that outside body shape. If that's not just right, they won't even stop to learn what a woman is like inside."

I glanced through the sliding glass door to where the men were talking. "Even if there are stereotypes about men being judged by their earning level, and women being judged by their bodies, at least men can work to improve their earning level. They can take courses, build skills, and take other steps." I looked down at my body. "Women are stuck with genetics and time. No matter what I do, each year I will get a year older. The younger twenty-something girls will undoubtedly seem more and more appealing in comparison."

I shook my head. "I still remember in high school, when a guy was talking about the band Heart. He was laughing that Nancy Wilson was the important part of the band, because she was blonde and slim. That her sister Ann was only there because Nancy made the others keep her." I sighed. "I remember being immensely upset. Here these women were both talented musicians, both at the very top of their game, and they were still being judged by their body shape. That's all this guy could see."

The men came back into the room and everyone returned to their stations. Paul fiddled a bit with the knobs. "How about we try something that everyone sings, to see if the mix is right?"

I called out, "How about 'Band on the Run'?"

Jason shook his head. "We don't do that, now that Todd is gone."

I sighed. It seemed we'd lost a number of my favorites when the lead guitarist had left the group. He'd married in May, and a month later he had resigned. Maybe there had been something to what Barry had said, that the act of changing roles in life brought along expectations. I still remembered a friend of mine, when we were in our twenties, who dated a guy who loved to go to strip clubs. My friend had reassured me that this was a "bachelor thing" and that once he became her husband he would of course change.

He hadn't. And undoubtedly he was surprised when she was upset. After all, they were the same people, with the same interests. Nothing had changed.

I thought about Mary, about the step she was about to take from a quiet student, a dutiful sister, an obedient girlfriend. She was going to expand into a new role, one where she could control and direct her own life.

Had someone been upset enough by that change to kill her?

Chapter 13

I took a sip of fresh lemonade before opening up my laptop on my back porch table. The sun was shimmering through the clouds, and a cardinal sailed across the yard, his wings a crimson flash against the deep green. The tomato plants were already taller than my head, and the squash leaves stretched larger than the proverbial dinner plate. It seemed as if we were only weeks away from a bounty of food.

The computer screen glistened into life, and I tapped at the keys. Our trip to meet Mary's family last night had not been exceedingly fruitful. Apparently the poor girl had been eager to put some space between her and her two brothers. But there had been another adult in Mary's life – one who had guided and supported her in her dreams. Both the rabbi and the brothers had talked about an art mentor.

I went to Google and typed in, "Mary Goldstein Wins Massachusetts Award."

There it was – the news article about Mary's success in 1984, edging out the many other competitors to take the top prize. I took a sip of my lemonade as I read my way through the praise for Mary's talents.

Aha.

Mary Goldstein attributes much of her success to her middle school art teacher, who now works at the high school Mary attends. "If it wasn't for Ms. Cecily Garman, I don't know if I'd be here today," explained Mary. "She is the one who encouraged me. She had me try oils, pastels, photography, and other media before helping me decide on watercolors. She believed in me. I owe her everything."

Surely, if Mary had owed Cecily everything, she would have let Cecily know what her plans were, even as she shut her brothers out?

I tried a fresh Google search. "Cecily Garman Worcester MA."

The first result popped on the screen, and I clicked. It was a press release from the Worcester Art Museum. Cecily Garman, holding a PhD in art history, had been hired six years ago to oversee their restoration department.

My eyes lit up, and I clicked over to the Worcester Art Museum's webpage. The title banner trumpeted the free admission for July and August, while a promo beneath it called for attention to their exhibit of Winogrand's "Women Are Beautiful" exhibition.

My shoulders slumped. The hours page indicated that they were closed on Tuesdays.

I glanced at the calendar. Tomorrow was free, and apparently their Wednesday hours were eleven to five. I grabbed a pen and wrote it in. Then I sent off an email to their contact link.

My cell rang, and I glanced at the screen while picking it up. "How are things going, sweetie?"

"Going well; lots of kids in the pool today," he answered. "Nice to see people out enjoying the fresh air. You?"

"I think I've tracked down Mary's art mentor. It's Cecily Garman. I'm going to the Worcester Art Museum tomorrow, and hopefully I'll get a chance to talk with her."

"You want me to come along? I'm sure I can rearrange a thing or two."

"No, I'm sure I'll be fine. It's the middle of an art museum. How much trouble could she cause?"

There was a pause, and my mind slid back to last November, to an elderly man who I had thought was sweet and kind. I had almost died that afternoon. I was only here now because of Jason's concern and fast action.

My voice was more serious when I spoke again. "Really, Jason, I will be fine," I reassured him. "I will make sure we talk somewhere public."

"You call me before and after," he stated, brooking no argument.

"I will, I promise."

He sighed. "All right, I suppose you're right. The chance of her doing something wild in the middle of an art museum is probably fairly slim." His voice eased. "So, going out with your friends tonight?"

"Yup, to the TGI Fridays at the Millbury mall. And when I get home, I want to watch that White Queen first episode on the DVR. It's set during the War of the Roses and is apparently similar to *Mists of Avalon*. It's about the women behind the scenes during a well-known historical period."

"Sounds good," agreed Jason. "Have fun tonight."

I had just about caught up with my inbox flood when it was time to head out. Luckily traffic was light, and I made it there in only fifteen minutes. The mall was infamous for its one way in, one way out. During the holidays the backup here could reach two hours or more. And now they were talking about putting a casino right next door? I could only imagine the kind of traffic woes that might generate. Apparently the Millbury town meetings were fairly intense, with a lot of questions on just how the casino would affect the town.

Geraldine and the others were already at the table when I came in, and she held up a wine bag with a helium balloon in the shape of a star tied to one handle. "In honor of your graduation!"

I blushed, accepting the gift. In my younger years I had dropped out of college after only one year, and I had regretted that decision ever since. Three years ago I had finally enrolled at Northeastern, determined to see this through. The advent of online courses had finally created an opportunity that worked well with my late night hours. Just three months ago I had finished the very last class.

I smiled at the group, taking my seat. "I still haven't received the official diploma," I reminded them. "That shows up in the mail in September."

Geraldine nudged me in the ribs. "Sure you don't want to go to that graduation ceremony?"

I vigorously shook my head. "And stand in front of tens of thousands of strangers, all to have someone hand me a piece of paper? No thanks. The party my mom is throwing for me on Saturday will be all the fun I could hope for. Besides, Jason's band will be playing."

Tanya leant forward. "Well, while we won't be able to make it to that, we wanted to have our own celebration with you. You deserve it."

The waitress came over. "Drinks?"

I glanced at the menu. "I'll have your Prosecco split."

One by one the other women followed suit, and in a moment we were toasting, laughing, and celebrating the achievement of a milestone.

Chapter 14

The weather was absolutely gorgeous as I drove up Route 146, and for a moment I thought of putting off the trip to the Worcester Art Museum, to call Jason instead and ask him to come kayaking with me. I shook my head. The murder might have happened twenty-nine years ago, but in the murderer's mind this revelation was fresh and new. They might be scrambling to cover tracks or invent alibis. The sooner I could talk to those involved, the more I might catch someone off guard.

Still, I looked wistfully at the puffy white clouds as I drove between the large windmill of Holy Cross and the flock of smaller ones around the Walmart parking lot. It was just a few more minutes before I was turning in to the Worcester Art Museum parking lot.

The building was large, sturdy, with its towering grey stone walls making it look like a vault for precious items. Which, of course, it was. A banner streamed down by the doors announcing their free admission, and I walked to them, slinging my camera over my shoulder. If for some reason Cecily was not able to meet me, at least I'd be able to take some photos.

The two women at the admission desk smiled as I approached. "What is your zip code?"

"01590," I told them. They handed over a small sticker for me to put on my dress.

I picked up a map. "I'm here to see Cecily Garman."

"Just one moment." The receptionist picked up a phone, pushed a few buttons, and spoke into it. "Someone to see you, Ms. Garman."

She nodded and replaced the phone in its cradle. "She will be out shortly. If you would wait by the mosaic, I'm sure it will be just a minute."

I nodded and walked forward into the main atrium. The space was gorgeous, with a pair of granite staircases down the back wall, and stone arches around three sides of the second floor. The center of the room was cordoned off, and it held a sixth century mosaic from Antioch. The work was probably twelve feet by twenty-four and held a variety of hunting scenes. I looked at the tigers, at the level of details in the animals. To think this had been done with tiny stones!

The sharp snap of heels on stone danced down the stairs, and a short, slender woman in a black suit with a matching skirt came toward me. She was in her sixties, judging by the creases on her face, but her hair was jet black and her eyes held hawkish focus to them. She drew to a stop before me and put out a hand.

"Cecily Garman. I heard you wanted to talk with me about Mary Goldstein?"

I nodded, shaking her hand. "If you had a few minutes, I would appreciate it."

"Absolutely," she chirped. "That girl was a prodigy. A next Van Gogh or Monet. I heard that they might have found her body. An absolute tragedy."

She glanced around her. "Maybe we could walk as we talk? That way you could see some of the museum. Much better than sitting in a stuffy office."

I smiled. "I would like that." I glanced to the left. "The Chapter House is always one of my favorites. Should we start there?"

She raised an eyebrow. "Ah, so I see you know our offerings. Certainly, lead the way."

The stone arches to the left side of the mosaic were different from the ones ringing the second floor. They were rougher, softer, and they led into an authentic French twelfth-century chapter house. This had been the one room in the monastery that the monks were allowed to talk in as they handled the necessary business of running the community.

I hushed, as I always did, as I walked into the room. It was perhaps double the size of my bedroom, with high, vaulted ceilings. Two columns in its center helped support the heavy stone. A fireplace to one side was flanked by stained glass windows, and a circular carving of Mary and Jesus hung over it.

I looked at the carving for a long moment. The victim had been named for that woman, and it seemed her life had also been beset by sorrow.

I turned back to Cecily. "You knew Mary well?"

She dropped her eyes. "Perhaps better than anyone else," she agreed. "Her brothers loved her, that was clear. They poured their energy into guiding her along a straight, narrow path." She gave a wry smile. "But Mary wasn't a joint to be welded or a pipe to be hammered into shape. She was gentle. She was full of rich creativity."

She stepped over to the stained glass. "When I first met her, she was entering seventh grade. She was like a timid mouse, huddling in a corner, barely willing to raise her hand." Her voice grew rough. "Mary's brothers had done that to her. Dropping her off at the school door each morning, picking her up immediately afterward, watching her every move. She couldn't have friends over or visit them. She couldn't participate in sports. Her life was to study, eat, and sleep. I think her only break was the temple services on Saturdays."

She nudged with her head. We walked out of the chapter house and around into the medieval room. The far wall held a medieval crucifix, with Jesus hanging in agony.

A movement to my right caught my eye. I turned – and then stared in surprise.

A pair of video screens hung there, about the size of a pair of side by side windows. The left one showed a woman in her sixties, from the waist up, completely nude. The right one showed a man in his forties, also from the waist up, also nude. Both of the figures had their hands by their waist and were silently writhing, as if in pain.

Cecily gave a small smile. "Intriguing, yes?"

I glanced around the room. The other items in here were all thoroughly medieval. A stone sarcophagus, a trio of small stained glass windows, and a life-sized crucifix.

And the writhing, naked people.

Cecily eyed the screens. "The artist is Bill Viola, and the title of the piece is *Union*. The video runs on a six minute loop."

The video's motion had clearly been substantially slowed down. It was as if the characters were clawing their way through molasses, as they struggled and stretched to slowly, painstakingly raise their hands up, to reach for something above them.

Cecily glanced at the crucifix. "The agony, the desperation for a better life, is a hallmark of medieval artwork. And well it should be, given the black plague and other calamities the people of that time period had to endure. Viola is giving us a modern take on that same emotion, with a medium more in line with how we now absorb information."

I looked at the woman in the video, her short, blonde hair frazzled out around her face, the wrinkles carved into her face, the sagging weight of her breasts. "Kudos to her for baring herself to the world like this," I murmured. "Our culture has gotten too beauty obsessed. You hear snide comments on the beaches if an older woman wears even a one piece swimsuit, never mind a bikini. It is as if an older body is somehow unfit to be seen."

Cecily chuckled. "You should hear some of the teen girls and boys who see this. Apparently they are bombarded with so many images of Hollywood-style nubile, sexy bodies that it's quite a shock to them to see what aging is really all about."

I nodded. "Maybe we need more of these types of exhibits, then. Help set better expectations and maybe a healthier acceptance of how actual bodies look."

I glanced again at the grimaces on their faces. "But maybe there could be a message of hope and joy in there somewhere. I think the world already has more than enough agony."

She nodded. "Mary was the same way. When she found her talent with watercolors, I tried to guide her through the traditional styles. We went along the Blackstone River to paint scenes there. We went out to the various lakes. We visited farmsteads. She dutifully painted red barns and golden fields of grain."

Cecily gave a soft sigh. "I know she wanted to please me, but as she stretched her wings, it was clear she craved more. In the autumn of 1982 she moved up to the high school, and I asked for a transfer. I wanted to be there. I wanted to see this caterpillar metamorphose, to become the brilliant, shimmering butterfly I knew lay within. I took her to art shows in Boston and New York City. I had her try painting cityscapes and urban scenes. Nothing seemed to click."

Her eyes went to the anguished faces before us, the artists' bodies stretched bare for the world to see. "And then came December."

My skin tingled. "What happened in December?"

Cecily's gaze was on the pain in the faces on the screens. "It was a few days before Hanukah began, and Mary disobeyed her brothers. She snuck out with a girlfriend to see *Sophie's Choice.* It had just opened at the movies – over where the Hanover Theater is now. The girls had heard it was sexy and about a woman with two lovers."

She shook her head. "Mary's face was just like that face before us, when she came in to see me the next day. She hadn't gone home – she'd called her brothers and told them she was sleeping over at her friend's house. The first time she'd ever done that. But she knew, if she had to go and face them, that she couldn't take the emotions. Even a full day later, it was as if her world had crumbled around her."

She twisted her fingers together. "I think it had been one thing to hear about the history of the war, dry and recited, in a safe classroom. The dates and people could seem far away. But to see the scenes played out on a large screen, the horror that was the concentration camps, ripped her world apart."

Her eyes grew distant. "We talked for hours that day. About life and death, about duty and sacrifice. About remembering those who were lost. And at the end, she knew absolutely what she wanted to do. She wanted to bring some small amount of closure and hope to the families of the victims. She wanted to do some small act to help them heal from the horrors of the Nazi campaign."

The couple before us was straining, reaching, and then suddenly the screen reset. They were at the beginning of their cycle again, hands low, the process beginning anew.

Cecily blew out a breath. "How about we go up to the second level? We have an interesting exhibition there, of Winogrand's photos.

I nodded, and we walked back out to the main atrium, going up the long sweep of stone steps to the upper floor. The photos were in a gallery to the left, and we stepped in.

I turned to Cecily. "How did her brothers feel about this new focus of hers?"

She crossed her arms. "I admit I was surprised, but they were actually supportive of it. Until then they had looked on her painting as frivolous, and they barely tolerated her time taken away from her studies. But now, they seemed to take it as a sign of her calling. They bought her a new easel and an expensive set of watercolors. As families expressed an interest in her portraits, the brothers would drive her to the houses for the interviews and meetings."

I looked over the photos before me in the gallery. The images were all black and white. They were like snapshots – unposed, unplanned, as if Winogrand had simply walked down a busy New York street and had hastily snapped a photo of a sexy woman in high heels.

"Hmmmmm," I said.

Cecily raised an eyebrow. "Oh, just wait."

We walked further along the exhibit, and I shook my head. If I had imagined what a "Women are Beautiful" exhibition would contain, I would have thought of an aging grandmother making pasta for her family, a tender mother caring for her infant child, or perhaps the classic beauty in a peasant farm-woman. But apparently Winogrand had a different take on the concept.

It seemed that every woman Winogrand photographed was between the ages of eighteen and twenty-two, was slender, and had a specific amount of curviness. In many of the photos the women were wearing skin-tight tops which clearly outlined every part of their breast's anatomy. In others, the photo had been taken at an angle to show glimpses of the women's underwear.

In one photo, a young woman, perhaps eighteen, leant forward to smile at something off-camera. A man near her took the opportunity to openly leer at her nearly bare breasts. In another photo, a woman wore a see-through top. A large crowd of men surrounded her, all staring with interest at her chest.

Cecily pointed to a photo ahead of us. "This one disturbs me more than the rest," she stated.

It was a beach scene. A woman in a bikini was to the right, walking toward the camera, with what appeared to be a concerned look on her face. But squarely center in the frame was a young girl in pigtails, perhaps nine, facing away from the camera. She was in a bikini. Her legs were spread in a V as she bent over to lay out her blanket. And the shadow of the photographer's head was visible at the bottom of the image. He was apparently standing right behind that bent-over young girl.

Cecily shook her head. "If I'd been that Mom, not only would I have charged at the photographer like an angry bull, but I would have broken his camera as well."

I pursed my lips. "I suppose he'd say that he's simply taking photos of real life. He's not posing the people. He's not dressing them. This is the way they're being seen by countless others."

Cecily nodded. She indicated a photo of a woman in a white feather dress, where the front was open nearly to her navel. The dress barely covered her nipples. "Winogrand didn't make this woman dress this way at the museum opening. She chose this dress. She went there willingly, wanting people to look at her body."

I looked at another photo, of a woman in a phone booth. She had a leg up, her foot resting on a support within the booth.

Winogrand had managed to find an angle which looked up her skirt. "And something like this?"

"I suppose he was warning people to be more aware of what they are showing to others. If a woman wears a dress and does not want her underwear to be seen, she should not hike her leg up above her knee."

I moved again to the photo of the young girl, bent over, with the shadow of a man's head looming behind. "And this? Should young girls not be allowed to wear bathing suits? Or to bend over?"

She frowned. "Maybe it is a warning for parents – that there are men out there who have perversions. It's an alert that parents should be aware of the danger and vigilant in protecting their girls from the predators."

I gave a wry smile. "Judging from the look on that mother's face, I think she got the message loud and clear."

Cecily's phone rang, and she glanced at it. "Excuse me a moment." She put the phone to her ear, and her voice became tender. "Hey there, sweetie. Yes, I'll be home for dinner. I wouldn't miss our anniversary. See you soon. Love you."

I smiled. "Congratulations. How long have you two been together?"

She pinkened. "We've been a couple for fifteen years, but only officially married in the summer of 2004. We made the plans as soon as Goodridge became official."

I smiled. "Good for you."

Cecily looked around the room and wrinkled her nose. "I think I've had more than enough of this exhibit. Up another floor?"

In a moment we were standing before *Waterlilies* by Monet. I gazed at the subtle shadings of aquamarine and mint green, at the delicate placement of the floating flowers.

Cecily nodded. "One of my treasures. The man was an absolute genius."

She waved to the left. "But this one was always one of Mary's favorites."

We went over to a large painting, perhaps four feet by six feet, of a gathering of people. The room they were in was white stucco with mint green highlights. The many men and women seated around the room wore Middle Eastern style outfits, with turbans on the men and shimmering gold jewelry on the women. There were lutes and tambourines, dancing and laughter.

Cecily's voice was low. "*Jewish Wedding*, by Renoir."

I looked at her. "Was Mary thinking of getting married?"

She twined her fingers together. "Once Mary's brothers approved of her watercoloring efforts, this museum became her safe haven. Any time she wanted to get away from them, she simply had to say she was coming to the museum. The brothers would drop her off and let her stay here for hours. They figured the place was like a fortress, and of course they were right."

Her eyes softened. "But they didn't figure on Xander. From what she said, he was staring at this very painting when she first found him. She asked him what he thought, and when he answered, it was the most insightful description she had ever heard. They talked for hours. He came back the next day, and the next, and soon it was love."

I looked at the painting, at the men in their turbans, at the sense of tradition and history. "Xander was a Congregationalist."

She nodded. "He was, indeed. From a family who took their faith in Jesus quite seriously."

"And I doubt Mary's brothers would have reacted much better," I mused. "They probably had a proper Jewish lad from the right family all lined up for her."

"Several," agreed Cecily. "They were just waiting for her to graduate from high school before moving on to that next step."

I shook my head. "Do you remember anything in particular about the time she vanished?"

She pursed her lips. "Well, Xander had just graduated from Sutton High. He was two years ahead of her. He was planning to go to Tufts, so he could stay local." Her mouth quirked. "I remember that they went horseback riding with some friends at a stables in Sutton. Poor Mary broke her arm fairly seriously.

But that girl was dedicated. The very next day she was back, cast and all, working on one of her projects. She had to hold her cast still, and move the paper beneath it, but she wasn't going to let her injury slow her down. She felt that strongly about the work she was doing."

"And then she was just gone?"

Cecily's eyes shadowed. "It was summertime, and there were so many things going on. She was going here and there meeting with families to discuss their departed loved ones. Newspapers were interviewing her. She was sneaking off with Xander. When I didn't see her, I figured she was just busy again. I figured when the school season started up again, she'd be back in class."

She let out a deep breath. "I was trying to give her her space. She'd worked so hard for this independence, for this freedom. I didn't want her to feel smothered."

"And then when school began?"

Her features sagged. "I was surprised when she wasn't in my class, and I went to ask the principal about it. He explained that she'd gone off to Germany to work on some sort of a government project. That it was an enormous honor." Her shoulders slumped. "I admit I felt hurt, that she hadn't told me about it herself. After all I'd done to help her, I felt abandoned. So I turned my back on her." She shook her head. "I should have followed up. I should have been the adult and gone past my petulance."

I looked again at the painting and all it had represented to Mary and Xander. My voice was a low murmur.

"Together we can make things right."

Chapter 15

When I was a teenager, I had ridden horses for two weeks each summer at Girl Scout Camp. But since those long-ago times, the most I had done was the occasional trail ride through autumn foliage. A twinge of envy coursed through me as I walked along the edge of the riding ring, watching the young girls canter with ease through the bright sunlight. They were medieval maidens, sure of themselves, enjoying a connection as old as history.

A sturdy woman strode toward me from the large, grey barn, smiling and waving her hand. Her dirty blonde hair was in a ponytail and hung to her waist over her denim shirt and jeans. Her handshake was firm and strong.

Her voice matched her build. "You must be Morgan," she stated, looking me over. "I'm Emma; I own this place. You said you wanted to talk with me about that accident back in 1984?"

"I'm surprised you remembered it so easily; it was a long time ago."

She leant on the wooden railing of the ring, her eyes sweeping to keep a careful eye on the girls and their steeds. "I remember everything that goes on with my horses and their riders," she stated. "Summer, 1984, girl with a broken arm. Had to be that artist type. She'd never been on a horse before, from the way she looked at poor Shadowfax. She thought he'd eat her whole, by the way she trembled."

I raised an eyebrow. "Shadowfax?"

She smiled. "Every horse has his or her own personality, and he definitely was the king of the stables. Elegant, smooth as silk, perfect for a beginner. No attitude nor feistiness. Should've been a cinch for her."

She shook her head. "It was that rabble that was with her, what caused the problem. All fired up from graduating and eager to prove themselves. They were cowboys, or knights, or I don't know what. Next thing I know, this blond kid launched into a gallop, nearly plowed into Shadowfax, and Shadowfax reared up to get out of the way." The corners of her mouth turned down. "She didn't hang on. Just let go. She was thrown right into the gate post."

"Do you know where they took her?"

Emma nodded. "UMass Memorial in Worcester. Her right forearm was snapped in three places. I remember because she was a painter, and she kept worrying about how it would impact her art. But her boyfriend stayed by her side. Promised her that she'd heal up right as rain."

I watched the girls chasing each other around the ring, their heads thrown back in laughter, their hair streaming in the wind. They were experiencing a sense of freedom coupled with control that few other activities brought. Somehow racing on a living creature was different from driving a car or riding a bike. It was more organic, more as if you were one with nature, soaring on a wind current, racing along a curling wave.

I glanced over at Emma. "Did you ever see her again?"

She shook her head. "Nope, and to be honest I didn't expect to. She hadn't seemed keen to come in the first place. After that experience I imagined that she wouldn't give it a second try. People can be like that. One wrong turn and they give up, even when something beautiful is just within reach."

I nodded in agreement.

Her lips drew into a line. "So do you think she's the one? The girl you found at the drive-in?"

I drew in a long breath, then nodded. "I'm going to go by the police station now and let them know what you told me. It should be easy enough for them to verify that the skeleton had matching breaks. I remember Jason telling me that hospitals hold onto their records for thirty years. We were close, here. The accident happened twenty-eight years ago. We found her just in time."

Emma put out her hand. "I'm glad to do my part to help that girl rest easy. She deserves it."

I shook her hand. "We all do."

It was only a short drive to get to the police station. It was next to the town hall on the central Sutton common, across the grass from the First Congregational Church. The small waiting room was empty, and an officer came promptly over to the glass window.

He gave a friendly smile. "Can I help you?"

I nodded. "I have news for the chief about the woman I found a few weeks ago at the drive-in. Did her right arm have breaks in three places?"

Sharp focus came into his eyes, and he picked up a notepad. "You're Morgan? What have you found out?"

I laid it all out for him, from the beginning. I imagined that the police had most of it, between their interviews and Jason's calls, but I figured it was better to repeat it all rather than risk leaving something out. By the time I was finished he had filled several sheets of paper.

He looked down at his notes, then back to me. "The Chief or a detective might want to talk with you later, to get more details on some of these items."

I nodded. "They know where to find me. I'm always happy to help."

He held up the pad. "Thank you. We'll definitely follow up on this." His eyes shadowed. "It will be nice to put a name to her and let her rest in peace."

I lowered my eyes. "She was going to invest her life into helping other families find closure. We owe it to her own family to do the same for her."

Chapter 16

I leant back in the black cast-iron chair, sipping my chardonnay, breathing in the fresh breezes coming off the eighteenth green. It was another gorgeous evening at Blackstone National and I did so enjoy their live music on the patio. Jason was on my right, and he raised his cabernet to me in a toast. Richard, the lawyer we'd chatted with at Pleasant Valley, was on my other side. His beer was half gone, and he was busily finishing off his plate of steamers.

He wiped his mouth on a napkin. "Last year you were able to bring peace to a group of men who never thought they'd find that again. And here you are, you've brought some small peace to brothers who thought their sister had run off on them. I'm sure her other friends appreciate knowing, as well. It is nice to be able to have that sense of wrapping things up." He laughed. "You two are a regular Nancy Drew and a Hardy Boy."

Jason raised an eyebrow. "A Hardy Boy," he murmured. "Ah, but which one?"

I smiled, taking a sip of my wine. "I admit, I was always partial to Shaun Cassidy."

He chuckled. "You were in your formative years when that show was out, you poor thing. Shaun's Joe Hardy was the impulsive one, the younger brother who would dive in without thinking." He smiled. "I always thought of myself more as Frank, the elder. He would think things through and map out a plan. Then he would tackle it with everything he had."

"Fair enough," I agreed.

A waitress walked by us with a chocolate brownie topped with a scoop of vanilla ice cream. My eyes longingly followed it. I really had to rein in my dessert habits here. Otherwise my yoga routine might get a bit more challenging, as my toes grew further from my outstretched fingers.

I glanced up at the waitress's face and stopped in surprise. "Cheryl?"

She looked down with a smile and it widened as she realized who I was. She turned to put the plate down before its recipient, then came back to me. "Morgan! It's great to see you."

I looked her over. When I had last seen her, the previous November, she had been a fully embroiled alcoholic. Her face had looked like a weathered apple, her posture had been hunched, her face sallow. She seemed to barely have the will to move from table to couch. She had grown up in the shadow of her beautiful older sister and somehow had never been able to escape it even after her sister's untimely death.

But now she was a woman reborn. Her eyes were bright and clear, her posture tall, and there was a spring in her step which came wholly from within.

I put out a hand. "You are doing wonderfully, I can tell. What is your secret?"

She pinkened. "It was you. I always meant to find you, to thank you."

I blinked in surprise. "Me?"

She nodded. "When we had our talk, you asked me why I never left the area. Why I never chased my dreams. I thought about that all that night, all the next week, and it struck home just how much I had gotten used to wallowing in my misery. I had created a rut for myself and couldn't even see beyond its narrow walls. I was trapped."

She tapped the side of her head. "I realized it was all in here, these barriers caging me in. So I joined AA. Three months later, I quit that job at the Publick House and found this one, closer to home. That gave me time to join the Whitin Community Center to try some Zumba and water aerobics. I won't say it's been easy, but I feel clearer. I feel my path opening up before me." A smile brightened her eyes. "It's been a long time since I could say that."

I stood and drew her into a hug. "I'm so happy for you. You deserve it."

She held my gaze. "Just that one talk with me got me thinking, and that was exactly what I needed. It helped me see the power of one kind word, of one gentle nudge. I'm trying to do my best to pay it forward."

I smiled. "I am sure you do it well."

She flushed, then nodded to us and headed to sweep up glasses at a nearby table.

A ball came sailing onto the green, bouncing a few feet from the hole. A ripple of applause came from the patio, and in a minute Derrick rode up on his cart, in a forest green polo with khaki shorts. He was joined shortly by two other men, and they putted in without much fuss. One of his friends took the cart off toward the parking lot, and Derrick waved at Richard as he approached the patio.

"Did you see that?" he asked heartily. "Nearly got it right in with that. The gods of golf are with me today. Got a birdie back on three and nearly had one on eight."

Richard raised his glass in a toast. "Seems it is your day indeed."

There was the heavy striding of feet behind us, and we turned. Xander was marching along the stone, his face crimson, his hands bunched into fists.

Jason half stood, putting himself between Xander and me.

But Xander wasn't coming for us. He drew to a halt close to Derrick's face, his gaze hot on him. His question spit from deep within him. "What did you do to her, you bastard?"

Derrick put his hands up in a show of innocence. "I read the news about Mary, and, man, I'm sorry to hear it," he vowed, his voice tight. "But I had nothing to do with it!"

"The hell you didn't," Xander snarled. "She was at that drive-in with someone, and you were drooling over her as if she was a fine cut of steak and you were ready to stick a knife in. Any time you were around her, you were finding an excuse to brush crumbs off her dress or to sweep hair from her cheek." His fingers flexed. "I know it was you making a move on her."

Derrick vigorously shook his head. "It wasn't like that," he promised. "Sure, I liked her. She was amazing. But she was never interested. She was hooked on you, Xander. She wouldn't give me the time of day."

Xander's face darkened. "You bet she wouldn't," he growled. "And so you attacked her! You took her away from me!" His balled fist rose to his hip.

Cheryl appeared as if out of thin air, smiling gently at Xander, gently putting a hand on his arm. "Xander, darling, it's been a while."

He looked up in surprise. "Cheryl? What? I haven't seen you around the docks in months."

She nodded. "My life took a little detour," she explained. "I have a lot to catch you up on. Come sit with me at the bar; I need to tell you all about it."

His eyes flashed back to Derrick. "But –"

"Oh, Derrick didn't have anything to do with Mary," she reassured him. "That wife of his, Melissa, has him on a leash tighter than a noose on a cattle rustler. She calls the bar constantly to check up on him. From what I hear from the regulars, she's been like that since high school. She never would have let him take another girl to a drive-in. Not without a nuclear meltdown following it."

The heat cooled from his cheeks. "Melissa did have a temper," he agreed. "And they were already getting serious by then. I remember, she was at that horseback-riding party we had."

Cheryl tucked her arm into Xander's. "See, nothing to worry about. Now come along with me. Did I ever mention …"

She deftly moved him around the other side of the table, keeping him clear of Derrick, and in a moment he was stepping safely inside the building.

Derrick shook his head, looking at the closed door. "Man, I didn't realize he'd go ballistic like that. He was with Mary thirty years ago! I barely remember the girls I was dating back then."

Jason's mouth quirked up. "Except Melissa, of course."

Derrick let out a barking laugh. "Sort of hard to forget her," he agreed. "Seeing as how she brow-beat me into marrying her." His cell phone buzzed, and he glanced down at it. "Speaking of which … I need to head out." He nodded down to us. "Good to see you all."

I looked after him as he walked to the parking lot. "Xander had seemed honestly upset when he came in after Derrick. Could it have been an act?"

Jason reached out to lay his hand over mine. "I suppose anything is possible, but I don't think so. He seemed truly upset, like a man reliving the loss of the woman he loved more than anything else in the world."

I squeezed his hand. "Hopefully something you will not have to experience," I reassured him.

His eyes shadowed. "I came very close."

I leant forward. "And then you saved me."

His eyes held mine, his lips came forward, and I drifted into a serene ocean, shimmering with warmth.

Chapter 17

I smiled as we eased into my mother's driveway. Paul's truck was already pulled up against the side of the house, and he, Meredith, and Adam were unloading the band's gear onto my mom's patio. She had an elegant, contemporary home, in dark wood, and the back yard was beautifully landscaped. She had put out several tables, a variety of chairs, and the flowers were in full bloom.

She came over to draw me into a hug. "Congratulations on your graduation," she smiled. "We are all so proud of you."

"It only took me twenty-seven years to earn this bachelor's degree," I teased. "Quite a bit of a break between my freshman and sophomore years. Most students just take off a year to go romp around Europe."

"Even more reason to celebrate," she agreed. "I'm just putting out the appetizers now!"

A pair of hummingbirds zinged by, and a few white, puffy clouds sailed across the sky. I helped her lay out the cheese, prepare the sangria glasses, and make ready for the fun.

It seemed like no time at all before the back yard was full of celebration. My best friend from high school arrived with a gorgeous bouquet of multi-colored daisies, in bright pink, vibrant blue, neon orange, and Crayola yellow. My Godparents were there, along with my Godsister, whom I'd grown up with from birth. My Dad arrived in his red convertible Miata with his girlfriend, Zelda. Meredith's voice rang out over the back yard, moving with ease from Adele to Zeppelin.

Simone from my writing group had brought her granddaughter, and the young girl was torn between desperately wanting to sing and being painstakingly shy. At last I grabbed my Godsister's hand and went up to the girl. "We'll sing backup," I promised. "And play maracas too. Come on up!" With that incentive, we soon had the entire audience singing along.

There was a break in the music as the main dishes were laid out. I poured myself another glass of the delicious sangria and sat alongside my mom.

"Thank you again for setting this all up," I commented. "It is wonderful to be able to see everyone. I'm sure I appreciate my degree far more than I would have back when I was younger. I understand the cost involved, and I absorbed the lessons far better. There was a context for what I was being taught. I could apply the information right away."

"It was my pleasure," she assured me. "And it's a treat to see everyone."

Her voice dropped. "And how are you doing with that poor girl you found? You said that you have confirmed who she is?"

I nodded. "Her name was Mary, and she was a pure soul. She used her artistic talents to help those recovering from the Holocaust."

My mother's gaze shadowed. "Good for her. As you know, my uncle died in one of those camps. He was not Jewish, but the Nazis were sweeping up everyone they could find at the time. My uncle was simply Ukrainian and able-bodied. They put him to work at hard labor; when he tried to escape, they sent him to prison." She looked down. "He never came out."

She sighed. "There was just an article on the topic of those camps, two weeks ago. It was carried in all the major newspapers. Forliti and Herschaft broke the story. It seems at least ten Nazis have been ordered to be deported from the US and are still here. Their native countries don't want them back, and we're not allowed to force them onto a plane to 'nowhere.' So they enjoy their old age, with all the benefits the US has to offer, and they never face any real justice."

I nodded somberly. "The Worcester Telegram carried that story, on July thirty-first. One of those men, Vladas Zajanckauskas, lives in Sutton."

She blinked in surprise. "Really? In your home town?"

I nodded. "It was back in 2007 that he was ordered deported. That's six years ago. But Lithuania doesn't want him back. So he gets to live here, a contented life, without any proper trial to examine the things he had done."

Her brow creased. "Maybe he was a desk clerk in an outpost in Africa. Somewhere far from the true horrors of the war."

I shook my head. "The written records clearly show his name on the list of soldiers assigned to the clearing of the Warsaw Ghetto," I explained. "Not only did he serve at Trawniki, which was a brutal extermination camp, but he was also sent to do the liquidation of the ghetto."

Her eyes went round. "And what is his counter to this?"

I ran a hand through my hair. "He agrees that he worked at Trawniki – but only as a bartender. He says that he never had the slightest idea of what went on at Trawniki, even though the location of the bar was right on the main square where the executions took place."

She pressed her lips into a line. "Even if he is somehow innocent, this should still be examined in a proper court of law. Over 300,000 people from that ghetto were exterminated. Most were killed at Trawniki – and most within a narrow two month time period. Even the most naïve of inhabitants should have noticed something. Those hundreds of thousands of people deserve to have this looked into."

I nodded quietly. "I agree. It seems sometimes that we're willing, as a society, to express outrage and horror if a puppy is abused – we can see and relate to that. But when something larger takes place, we seem more likely to keep it at arm's length. Maybe we feel it couldn't really have happened."

Zelda came over to join us. "It relates to Dunbar's Number," she explained. "The average person tends to maintain close social contact with perhaps one hundred and fifty people. Our brains are designed to care about our immediate social group. When the numbers get larger, the cognitive work shifts to another part of our brain. It no longer feels so immediate."

My mother nodded. "I ran into that when I was a journalist. If I wrote about a young woman who was brutally attacked, the donations would come pouring in. Readers could relate to that woman. They could imagine themselves in her place, or perhaps their sister or daughter. The injury was relatable." She shook her head. "But when someone writes about the nearly 500,000 people slain in Darfur, or up to a million people in Rwanda – in just a half year! – the human mind has trouble absorbing it. The excuses start, to distance ourselves from it."

Zelda sighed. "Yes. People think that somehow the victims deserved it. Or that the culture is 'less developed' and therefore it's natural for the violent behavior to happen. Or that there isn't much we could do about it anyway. There's even the thought that 'we should take care of our own first' – as if people near us are deserving of love, but those beyond arm's reach are on their own."

My mom nodded. "There's even a time factor, too. Some feel that the Holocaust is in a far distant past, like the Civil War. That whatever went on doesn't matter any more."

Zelda's face hardened. "Brutality always matters. It should be remembered, so we do not have it happen again. Maybe if we had cared more about the Holocaust, we would have taken stronger action, as a world society, when Rwanda and Darfur were going on."

My mother's brow creased. "And instead, in the US alone, we spend eight billion a year on cosmetics. Imagine what we could do if we spent that money on peace related projects. Imagine the lives we could save and the standard of living we could develop for everyone."

I leant forward. "And that would then help all societies to improve. It would mean less money was spent on supportive systems for those in jeopardy. It would also mean we'd have more consumers to buy goods, so we could have more jobs for everyone. It would be a true win-win."

The band moved back onto the stage, and a hummingbird zipped by me. I smiled. "For today, at least, we can celebrate community, joy, and the hope of a brighter future."

Chapter 18

I sipped at my wine, watching the hummingbird hover over the perch on my back feeder. It lit, cautiously, on the small red support before tucking its beak into the plastic opening to sip.

The result came up on my laptop screen, and I scrolled through the images. Mary had indeed been prolific in her few years of projects. There were a number of her paintings posted online. I was touched by their beauty. One was a young boy in a jaunty cap. Another was an elderly woman, her face creased with wrinkles. In each case it seemed as if the person was vibrantly alive, a smile on his cherubic lips, a sparkle in her gold-flecked eyes.

I clicked through to the details of the images. Often there was a story about the person in question, rich with historic details. In other cases it was just the image itself with no background information.

There was an elegant, middle-aged man in a crisp brown suit, and I selected him, intrigued.

Welcome to the Marcus Interon Auction House.

I sat back, my brow creasing. It made sense, I suppose. People passed away. Estates were sold. Eventually some of Mary's paintings would end up passing from hand to hand.

I looked through the listing for any details about where the painting had come from.

Provenance – Painting was supplied for sale on August 17, 2013. Owner is Cecily Garman, the mentor of the painter.

I blinked. That was yesterday. Cecily had put the painting up for sale yesterday – just when the death had become public knowledge. And, judging by the bids on the page, Mary's death was good news for those who owned her artwork.

Jason came out onto the back porch, coming over to pat me on the shoulder. "How are you doing?"

I looked up at him. "Fancy a ride over to the Worcester Art Museum?"

A half hour later we were mounting the steps to the granite building, and my eyes went automatically to the medieval chapel beyond the information desk. With any luck, I'd be able to spend a few minutes there before she came down to talk with us.

The desk woman looked up. "Zip code?"

"01590," I answered automatically. "But we're here to see Cecily Garman."

"Oh, she isn't here," answered the clerk. "I know, because we were going to go to lunch. She had to run over to Higgins to oversee something about the upcoming transfer."

I looked up at Jason. "Change of plans."

He grinned. "An afternoon at Higgins? Twist my arm!"

Higgins armory was opened in 1931 and contained a mind-boggling amount of medieval arms, armor, and other historical material. It was reputed to be the largest collection outside of Europe. And it was right here. In no time at all we were parking outside the three-story glass and steel structure.

We bought our tickets and went up the stairs to the main hall. I could be content here for hours, and on many occasions I had been. It was stunning to look at one of these suits of armor and to think of the knights who had worn it. These were not just leather jackets. They were intricately crafted works of art, made of hundreds of interlocking pieces, all to protect a single person.

I heard a familiar voice down the hall and turned. Ah, there she was. Cecily was talking to a man in his thirties with a pony-tail partway down his back. They were gesturing to a trio of pikes hanging on a wall.

I waited until their conversation finished and the man headed back toward the stairs. Then I moved over.

She looked up in surprise. "Morgan! Funny to meet you here. Are you a fan of Higgins?"

I nodded. "Indeed I am. This is my boyfriend Jason. We come here often."

She looked around her. "A shame that it has to move, but the Worcester Art Museum is of course happy to help out. We will put our team to work restoring the pieces, and soon they will be back on display, better than ever."

I nodded. "Or some might be auctioned off."

She shook her head. "We don't have any intention of separating out the collection," she countered. "It will all be entrusted to us, and we will care for it as a unit."

I raised an eyebrow. "Unlike Mary's works?"

Her brow creased in confusion, and then she paled. She glanced around. There were only a trio of college students at the jousting display, examining the long lances.

Her voice dropped low. "Those paintings were personal gifts, from Mary to me," she insisted. "They were practice works that she did not feel were up to being sold. She gave them to me for my own pleasure."

"And it was your pleasure to hold onto them until her body was discovered, and then to promptly sell them? Surely, for most people, their first instinct on hearing of a death is not to run to an auction house."

Cecily paled further. "It wasn't like that," she insisted.

"Oh?"

She looked down for a long moment. "I have Lyme disease," she admitted at last. "I got it in the early eighties, but back then doctors didn't know much about Lyme. They told me my symptoms were all in my head." She shrugged. "Now I have heart palpitations, chronic arthritis, you name it. Some days it's a struggle just to get out of bed."

She sighed. "I didn't want to sell the paintings. They held great emotional meaning for me. But you get to a point in life where ..." She rolled her hand. "The paintings were decorative. I have images of them on my computer and can look at them any time I wish. But my health – that is critical. I can live without the paintings. I need my medication."

I nodded in understanding. "I'm sorry to hear about your illness."

She shrugged. "At least now they know what it is," she pointed out. "For decades they had me convinced I was imagining it all. I went to doctor after doctor, and each one told me it was all in my head. They nearly had me convinced, too."

She looked up at the suit of armor before her. "Once, things were simple. You saw who your enemies were. They stuck a sword at your chest. Either you deflected it or you didn't. Now, our threats are far more sinister."

I gave a wry smile. "They had baffling diseases back then, too," I pointed out. "The Black Plague wiped out large populations and the doctors of the time had no idea why. Each generation has its own challenges to face."

She sighed. "I suppose you're right." She turned to face us. "In any case, there will be one painting I'll never sell. Mary explicitly asked me to hold onto it. It's an evening scene of the Blackstone River by the Singing Falls in Sutton. Dark ochres and vermilions. So I'll always have that." She gave a soft smile. "As if I need anything physical to remember her talent. I can close my eyes and see each painting she created, as clear as these maces in front of us. Her work was like that. The faces of those lost in concentration camps seared into your soul."

I nodded in agreement. "She helped preserve memories which should never be forgotten."

She blinked, and a hollow look came to her gaze. "There isn't any painting of *her*."

I glanced at Jason. "What?"

Cecily's shoulders slumped. "All the images she did for others, and there isn't one of her. I should have had her do a self-portrait. I never even thought of it. I thought there'd be more time. So much more time …"

I gently patted her on the shoulder. "We all tend to think that. But time is fleeting – the glimmering of a cloud-white dandelion seed which spins in the air, and then swirls on a gust of wind, lost forever from view."

Chapter 19

The cemetery service wasn't until three, so Jason and I were taking a walk through Purgatory Chasm to check on the frogs. We were in luck. The weather was stunning, and we were at the stream down by the Little Purgatory path.

I smiled with delight. "Look at these green frogs!" There were a number of them in a variety of stages of coloring. Some were all green, some were all brown, and a scattering of them seemed to have been dipped in paint, so sharp was the line between their green and brown halves.

I took a step back to get a better angle for my photo and laughed in delight as an American Toad hopped out from beneath me. "These little suckers are everywhere," I teased.

"Here are some bullfrogs," pointed Jason. "You can tell because the ridge on the side of their head wraps around their ear drum, rather than sailing straight over it."

I dutifully aimed the camera and got a number of photos of them.

He dropped to a knee. "And look! A wood frog too! We've hit nearly half the frogs in Massachusetts!"

I looked at the small, delicate frog, painted in shades of tan and darker brown. "What a cutie."

We walked along the path to the small bridge. I looked down into the pond. "Do you remember when we stood here last November?"

He nodded, wrapping his arms around me. "You thanked me for finding you."

I smiled, drawing him in. "I thank the universe every day for that," I murmured.

And then his lips met mine.

* * *

I was pleased to see a fairly large group of people at the far reaches of Sutton Cemetery. It seemed, even so many years later, that Mary's efforts had been appreciated. Men and women of all ages milled around in the warm afternoon sun, talking in low murmurs. Jason took my hand as we approached the group.

The two brothers, wearing black suits, stood near the rabbi. They talked quietly for several minutes. Then the rabbi turned to the assembled group.

"Gather around, please," he called out, his rich voice carrying easily across the cemetery.

I was impressed by his sermon. Clearly he had researched Mary thoroughly. He covered everything from her childhood love of cinnamon red-hots to her explorations of art styles. He talked about how she felt lost, and then discovered her calling in life. He reminded us that all life is precious and that our time on Earth is far too short. We should treasure each day we have and use our time wisely.

He turned to the side, and Cecily stepped forward, wearing a deep grey suit. She turned to the crowd.

"My name is Cecily, and I had the privilege of mentoring Mary during her brief, shining life. Yes, the young woman had natural talent – but it was more than that. She had the drive to use that talent for good. So many times people with a gift squander it, or use it for purposes which cast a shadow. Mary reminded us that there is always a way to do good with the abilities you are graced with."

She looked around the assemblage. "Each and every one of us has something we are talented in. Maybe it's cooking or sewing. Perhaps it's networking or helping people to smile. Whatever your talent is, give it thought. It is part of what makes you unique and special. Find a way to bring light into our world with it."

Her eyes glistened with tears. "That would be a fitting legacy to Mary's memory." She bowed her head and stepped back.

The two brothers stepped forward, and Ephraim spoke. "It means a lot to us that you all came here to help see Mary off. Cecily is right. Mary had a dream to help bring closure to families in pain. She was going to use her God-given talents toward that goal. If you are inspired by Mary, then look through your own skills. Examine your own talents. See how you might use those to help others in need."

Barry nodded. When he spoke, his voice was hoarse. "Thank you all for coming. God bless you."

The crowd murmured in response, and then the group stretched, expanded, as people began heading back to their cars.

A couple moved toward us in the gentle surge. I blinked, then smiled. It was Derrick, Xander's high school friend, hand in hand with a slender woman with pale brown hair to her shoulder.

I waved. "Derrick! It was good of you to come."

He wrapped an arm around the woman's waist. "This is my wife, Melissa."

I put my hand out. "Melissa, it is lovely to meet you."

Her shake was gentle and warm. "Likewise. Derrick has told me so much about you both. It's nice to finally meet you in person."

There was a strong movement going against the stream to my left, and I turned in curiosity.

It was Xander, in jeans and a dark green t-shirt, his eyes blazing with heat. He pushed his way through the departing guests, swirling them like a flooded brook, driving hard toward the brothers.

The two men saw him coming, and their shoulders immediately drew tight; their faces went red with fury.

Xander had barely drawn up to them before Barry's voice rang out, sharp with hostility. "How dare you come! You desecrate this ceremony with your presence. You're the reason she's dead!"

Xander's fist raised high in Barry's face. "Me? It was you two, acting like prison guards from the time she was little, who destroyed her life! She could barely breathe without one of you looking down her throat! Whatever mess she got into, I know you two drove her into it!"

Barry's jaw tightened. "Our Mary was a good Jewish girl. She was all a brother could dream of. And then you tainted her. You fouled her!"

Derrick let out a strong exhale, then strode over to come up alongside Xander. "Come on, Xand," he urged, "they're not worth it. We know how they rode Mary, but that's in the past now. Today is about Mary and letting her rest in peace. We can deal with the brothers later. Let's go to the dock and talk about Mary. You know she used to love it there."

Xander's gaze stayed hard on the two brothers, but after a moment his shoulders slumped. His gaze moved to the opening in the ground, to the polished coffin which waited to be lowered within. He looked at it for a long moment, seemingly lost in another time. Then, at last, he nodded.

"She did love the dock," he agreed. "Sure."

Derrick glanced back at his wife, and she made a waving motion. "I'll find my way home," she called. "Go on, take him."

He gave a small smile, and then he looked to Xander. They strode side by side off toward the street.

I moved toward the brothers. They were glaring after Xander and Derrick, half looking like they might pursue the two men. I gave a low cough to draw their eyes back to me. "I just wanted to say how sorry I was for your loss."

Barry visibly gathered himself back from whatever fantasies he was spinning in his head, undoubtedly involving him landing on Xander and pummeling him into a pulp. "Right, yes, I appreciate it greatly, Morgan. Both of you, for coming to the ceremony."

"It was a lovely ceremony," I encouraged. "Very fitting to all she had accomplished."

Ephraim tucked his hands into his pants pockets. "She could have done so much more," he murmured. "So very much more." He glanced toward the street. "And that boy, as much as he caused trouble, was just a passing infatuation in any case. All teen girls go through that phase. I'm sure in the end that she would have focused wholly on her art – on the purpose God gave her those talents for." His gaze unfocused. "She would have been the glowing light which inspired countless others."

I looked out at the stream of departing cars. "She *has* inspired them," I reminded him. "Even all these years later, her influence is still felt."

Barry and Ephraim glowed at that, a kindle returning to their gaze. Barry nodded. "Yes, it is."

Chapter 20

Jason pulled the car over in the parking area before the Salt Pannes Wildlife Observation Area. The bright aroma of Plum Island Sound drifted in the open windows, and the marsh spread out before us, filled with the bobbing, striding shapes of semipalmated sandpipers. The delicate birds dove their slender beaks into the mud as if the most delicious of treasures lay just beneath the orange surface.

I put my wide-brimmed hat on my head and climbed out. In a moment Jason was beside me, camera over his shoulder, tucking an arm around my waist.

His voice was warm in my ear. "Gorgeous weather we've been blessed with."

I gave him a nudge. "It is your eighteenth anniversary with the rangers," I pointed out, "and we drove ninety minutes to get up here. The Gods of Nature want to make sure your trip to Plum Island is as wonderful as possible."

I drew my eyes across the beauty of the sound. A great blue heron was statue-still to the far left, his eyes focused on the water before him. In the far distance was the brilliant chalk-white of an egret.

I spoke without turning my gaze. "Have you ever thought about requesting a transfer up here?"

"To Parker River? It's certainly a gorgeous location. I love to visit." He gave a soft shrug. "But I prefer the mossy depths of forests, the secluded ponds and lakes." A smile drew to his lips. "And of course, now, it would be too far." He raised an eyebrow. "Unless you were thinking of moving?"

I shook my head. "I love it in Sutton," I stated with a smile. "Singletary and Manchaug are just the right size for kayaking. Purgatory and the Sutton Woods hold a great mix of trails for hiking." I leant my head against him. "And besides, all the hummingbirds come back to me year after year. The phoebes like their nest in the eaves. If someone else took over the house, who knows what they'd do? They might drive away the frogs and squash all the spiders!"

He chuckled at that, then pressed his lips to my forehead. "It's settled, then."

A short drive down the road and we were at the North Pool overlook. We held hands as we made our way to the side of the water. A flock of Canada Geese nestled contentedly on the far shore, basking in the sun, while swallows swooped low over the ripples.

I gave his fingers a squeeze. "Some people would be looking for Champagne and filet mignon on an anniversary like this," I teased him.

His eyes were deep as he turned to look at me. "Do you mind?"

I brought a hand up to lace into his hand. "Not one bit."

Our lips met, and I was very glad that we had the stretch all to ourselves for a long while.

At last we moved along to the observation tower. There were a scattering of other visitors here, moving quietly, taking photos or murmuring to each other in a hush normally reserved for great cathedrals. We made our way up the metal stairs, then stopped at the top to lean against the railing.

I sighed in contentment. There was a sleek, black cormorant diving into the depths. A pair of swans paddled serenely, their white bodies shimmering against the blue. A pair of ruddy brown ducks poked around in the grasses by the distant shore. I pointed them out to him.

"What do you think those are?"

He peered for a while, then shook his head. "I'll try to get some photos, and we can take a look later on."

Then we were walking side by side along the Marsh Loop trail, and we were completely alone. The grasses on either side of the boardwalk were up over our head. A low whooshing noise sung through the green, moving wall as the breeze came in off the sound.

A chime on my phone shimmered as we stood on the overlook of the Dune Loop. I looked down with a sigh. "It's my half hour warning. We need to start back to my writing group."

He pressed a kiss to my forehead. "That is just right," he agreed. "I imagine you're starving – you only had that protein shake for breakfast. And I can get some shopping done."

I raised an eyebrow. "Oh?"

He smiled. "You mentioned a special dinner. I need to gather up some supplies."

"You don't have to do that."

His eyes twinkled. "Technically, I don't have to do anything at all," he pointed out. "That's the beauty of free will. So I absolutely *want* to make us a delicious dinner and to enjoy a relaxing evening with you by my side."

I leant against him. "Then, by all means, let us head on out."

* * *

Sometimes our writing group was small, with just one or two people joining me for the afternoon. At other times we completely filled the eight-person table. Today there were four already present as I slid into my spot. The waitress came by just after I did. "Merlot?"

I nodded. "And a house salad with ranch," I added.

Anne handed over a brown bag which had a rounded cork poking out of its top. "Congratulations, Morgan."

Simone turned. "Oh, yes, congratulations on Jason's anniversary!"

Anne smiled. "Actually, this was for her graduation from college, but it can serve double duty."

I took the bag. "Thank you very much. This will come in handy tonight!"

The waitress returned with my drink and the salad. "Let me guess. Salmon."

I nodded, chuckling. She went off to add my order in to the others.

Anne turned to me. "I saw the obituary for the girl you found, Mary Goldstein, on the Telegram website this morning. Seems like she was quite a talented young woman."

I nodded. "I wish there was more of a chance of finding out what happened to her. But the odds are against us. Did you know in the US there are over 300,000 cold cases – people who were slain and we don't know by whom – just since the 1950s? And there are also 40,000 bodies who have not been identified. We might think we are a modern, technologically advanced society, but we still have some enormous gaps in how we connect the dots."

Anne nodded. "My PhD involved a great deal of lab work, and while we have come a long way since my research, there's still a long way to go. Yes, we certainly can do much better than our previous generation could. Just a few weeks ago CNN ran a report about the 'Oldest cold case ever solved' – about a child's murder in 1957. I'm sure Maria Ridulph's family is grateful to have that closure. But for most families, it never comes. Once a death is over a few weeks old, chances are slim of new evidence coming to light."

Simone sighed. "Much of it is due to the malleable nature of our mind," she pointed out. "I see this all the time in my hypnosis work. Someone might feel strongly that they saw a suspect in a red sweater. But if they are exposed to enough images and discussion of a man in a black shirt, they actually begin to believe they saw a black shirt. What is real in our memories is not carved in stone. It is soft and fluid, like a watercolor painting."

I took a sip of my merlot. "That is what Jason has been telling me, from his discussions with the police. It's not that they want to ignore the case. They care about Mary very much." I gave a soft shrug. "But it was decades ago. We don't even know what specific day she died on. So even if we wanted to ask her boyfriend, or her brothers, or her art mentor, 'where were you on the night of …' – we can't. And who could remember that kind of detail?"

I rolled my shoulders. "There are three breaks on her arm, but we know where those were from. The stables and brothers confirm that accident. There's no other clear sign of what killed her. There is only a skeleton now, and despite my fondness for the *Bones* TV show, I'm just not sure in real life that forensic science can find tiny nicks in bones to prove cause of death. So what does that leave us?"

I sighed. "Maybe her boyfriend was upset she was leaving for Germany. Maybe her brothers were. Heck, maybe her mentor was grumpy that this young protégée was blazing into a glorious future, with a bountiful grant, and never even said a word of thanks."

Anne raised an eyebrow. "What grant?"

"That was what caused all the commotion," I explained. "Mary had been awarded a massive grant from the German government. She was going to help them commemorate the victims of the Holocaust."

Anne's eyes crinkled in confusion. "That wasn't mentioned in the obituary."

I turned to her, baffled. "Surely they would have talked about it," I insisted. "It was one of the crowning achievements of her short life."

She shook her head. "I'm very sure. There was no mention of a grant at all."

Simone leant over. "Where did you hear about this grant?"

I closed my eyes, thinking back. "The rabbi. It was the rabbi who first mentioned it to me. But I also talked about it with Mary's mentor and with her brothers. So it wasn't a secret."

Simone's eyes were serious. "But was it real?"

I looked between them. "Maybe it's time to find out."

Chapter 21

Juliet gave a long, steady *mrrroowwwlll* at my side, and I absently reached down to pet her. It felt as if I had been at my computer all day long – and that was fairly close to the truth. My email had backed up, my to-do list had grown by leaps and bounds, and it was only the hummingbird feeder at my window that kept me sane. The sun shone, glorious, against the white *Hydrangea grandiflora* bush right outside my window. The hummingbirds occasionally stuffed their long snouts into the blossoms, but I wasn't quite sure if they actually got any nectar from that. It seemed they liked our sugar-water concoction much more. Maybe they were eternally hopeful that the hydrangea would yield something tasty.

I popped another Triscuit-and-cheddar combination into my mouth as I typed. I knew this wasn't exactly healthy for me – but for some reason it was my fall-back choice when I was hungry and had to keep working. Slice up a few squares, pour out a few crackers, and I was set. I needed to figure out something else to use to soothe my hunger pangs. Not right now, though.

Despite my attempts to focus on the email questions, my mind kept circling back to the question of the grant. It had seemed common knowledge amongst Mary's close circle. But why wouldn't it have been mentioned in the obituary? If Mary had been my sister, that grant would have been something I prominently mentioned. I had tracked down the Telegram article myself this morning, and Anne had been correct. The Massachusetts art award was there, as well as Mary's association with the Temple and her many projects. However, the grant was nowhere.

Stade.

The thought flashed to me, suddenly, that perhaps I had a way to investigate this. Back in 2003, I had gone to Stade, Germany with my father. This medieval town was on the most northern coast of Germany, up against Denmark. Our family traced to there in the 1400s, back into the earliest days of records. Stade was a walled city, a beautiful location of post and beam construction. I had enjoyed my trip there immensely. One of the contacts we had made there was involved, somehow, in the German government.

I dug through my email archives and tracked down the person's name. Johannes Waller. It was a full decade later, but I took a chance. I sent him an email detailing the situation, asking if he could look into it.

To my surprise, a response pinged back only fifteen minutes later.

Out having dinner with family. Delighted to hear from you. Absolutely will look into it over the coming days.

Chapter 22

I gazed in contentment at the acrylic painting of water lilies, marveling in the dappling of light on water. I had just seen Monet's interpretation of a similar scene, done in oils, when I visited the Worcester Art Museum a week ago. Now I was at a much different venue – the Milford Cable TV studio. The gallery was showcasing local artists from the Blackstone Valley Art Association. The beauty shown was just as powerful. In the background, music from a local band drifted along the hall as they warmed up for their recording.

Jason came up next to me, handing me a shallow, plastic glass of white wine. "Frank does a good job," he commented. He nodded his head at the next painting to the right. "I like this one a lot." It was an autumnal scene of a pond with dappled foliage and green pines under shimmering blue skies. The foreground held a pair of birch trees. Only a few burnt orange leaves clung to the twisting branches.

A deep voice came from behind us. "Thank you, I appreciate it."

We turned, and I smiled up at the man. He was in his mid-sixties, tall, with white hair and a friendly smile. I put out my hand. "You must be Frank. I'm Morgan, and this here is Jason."

He shook our hands, then looked down the corridor. "Do you have any art here?"

I shook my head. "Unfortunately, I missed the deadline for this round," I explained. "I did submit a few photos to the last exhibit, and I'm hoping to be more on top of things for the upcoming one. Still life and abstract, I believe the theme is."

He nodded. "So you had some water pieces to use for this?"

I smiled widely. "Jason and I love kayaking. I have directories full of images of the local lakes and ponds." I ran my eyes down the collection of paintings and photos. "Still, it looks like we had more than enough for the show."

I looked up at his water lily image. "I've been dabbling with watercolors recently. I've seen such beautiful results that other members have created." My smile turned wry. "I seem to make puddles of color, mostly."

Frank chuckled. "That is how it always begins," he reassured me. "Just keep practicing, and you'll get the hang of it. You learn to think in reverse. You paint in the backgrounds first – the blue sky, the dapples of the water. And then you paint the foreground over it." He looked up at his autumnal landscape. "Some people think watercolors are unforgiving, but it's not true at all. Acrylic ends up being far more transparent, in terms of seeing the under-layers. With watercolor, you could do a sketch, and start painting in one direction, and then change your mind. You could create an entirely new atmosphere by painting over sections of the old."

I looked at him in surprise. "I had no idea. I thought watercolors were like stained glass – that you could always see through the top layers down to the lower layers."

"Certainly you can create that effect if that's your aim, but it's not your only option. It all depends on the paints you use and the technique. Your end result would probably be darker than these here, for example. You'd need stronger colors in order to hide what lay beneath."

I looked over at Jason. "A darker than normal painting."

He nodded. "Maybe we should have a talk with Cecily, about that special painting Mary wanted her to keep."

I looked back at Frank. "If someone did this – created an alteration on top of a base painting – would there be any way to see what the original had been? To strip off just the top layer of covering paint?"

He tapped his finger to his lip in thought. "It might be done."

The first notes of "Bitter Sweet Symphony" by The Verve sounded, filling the hall, and I smiled.

Chapter 23

The world shimmered with beauty. I was in Warrior II pose on my back porch, surrounded by jalapeño plants, tomato plants, my tea rose with a single crimson bloom, and a large, white gardenia. Juliet sprawled on the first step of the porch stairs, lounging in the early afternoon sun. A tan dragonfly was perched on the right post, a speckled grey tree frog was tucked on the railing to the left, and a daddy long legs watched me placidly from his nook on one of the tomato plants.

Life was serene.

I turned each hand so the palm was facing up, rather than down, and I arched my back to look up at the sky as I rotated into Reverse Warrior II.

And stopped.

The sun was just at the point in the sky where it was shielded by the two large oaks on the right side of the house, but the rest of the sky glowed Persian blue with cottony white clouds drifting in occasional dollops. Ringing the hidden location of the sun, in a full circle for as much as I could see, was a faint, shimmering rainbow.

A sun halo.

I reached over and grabbed my cell off the closed lid of the grill, aiming it at the sky. A click, and the image was sent off to Jason. He was off leading a hike to the west, and he could be in a treed-in location. This might give him some incentive to get out into the open.

Then I sunk back into my routine.

Marjaryasana – Bitilasana - Setu Bandha Sarvangasana ...

Savasana.

Namaste.

I picked up the cell, glanced at the display, and smiled. There was a note from Jason.

So glad you saw it. Didn't want to disturb your yoga. Namaste, my love.

* * *

It seemed no time at all before crimson clouds were stretching across the sky and we were pulling into the Blackstone National parking lot. I could hear the acoustic guitar music as we walked to the patio, and there was a table open for us. We settled down, side by side, facing out over the eighteenth green.

A pair of men walked up to the tee box, and I leant forward. "Isn't that Derrick and Xander?"

Jason looked over, then nodded. "Indeed it is."

I smiled. "I'll be right back." I smoothed down my ivory dress, then walked down the small hill to the side of the green. A trio of men were sitting nearby in the Adirondack chairs laid out for spectators. One of them nudged his friends. "It's an angel!"

I chuckled. Hopefully I would be a good omen for the two golfers and not cause them to triple-put in front of the watchers.

Derrick's ball bounced up onto the green, only a few feet from the hole. Xander wasn't as lucky. His sailed off into the small stand of trees on the right hand side.

The pair hopped into their cart and drove up to the hole. Derrick strode over, smiling at me. "My good luck charm," he called out. "I might win this night yet."

Xander had located his ball and hunched over a small hill. He swung, and the ball came vaulting out, landing at the edge of the green. His face was surly as he came up to his ball.

Derrick stood back as Xander positioned himself. His first putt missed by several inches. The second stopped a foot short. The third finally got in.

The Derrick moved over, tapped his ball in, and smiled. "You owe me ten," he joked.

Xander pulled out his wallet, yanked out the bill, and handed it over. "I'll return the cart," he growled, turning his back on us.

Derrick looked up at the patio. "You here with Jason?"

I nodded. "Care to join us?"

"Sure thing," he smiled. We walked up the hill, and in a moment he was shaking Jason's hand.

Derrick settled down opposite us. The waitress came by. "Pair of Sams for me and Xander," he called out. She nodded and left.

Jason patted my shoulder. "I got you a chardonnay."

"Sounds good," I grinned.

Derrick leant over. "I know Xander is rough around the edges, but for both of us, thank you for finding Mary. You did a world of good with that. He was convinced for years that she had run off on him."

I put my hand over Jason's. "I can't even imagine how much he was hurt by that," I murmured. "It must have eaten away at him all this time. He thought she was out there somewhere, not even wanting to touch base to let him know how she was doing. Hopefully knowing the truth brings some small amount of closure."

Xander came up to the table, settling into his chair. In a moment the Sam Adams arrived, and he took down a long swallow. He looked over to Derrick, and a small smile eased onto his lips. He held up his glass. "Like old times, eh?"

Derrick touched his glass to Xander's. "Seems it's a bit harder to hit those long drives," he grinned.

Xander's smile grew, and he nodded. "I did miss it, though. Even with the sand traps and lost balls, it's good to be back out on the course. Thank you."

"Any time," replied Derrick.

By the lightness spreading through Xander's face, I had a sense that a rift was finally, gently, being mended.

Chapter 24

The phone was ringing. I blinked my eyes blearily awake and rolled over to look at the clock. 10:24am. Who in the world would be calling me this early? And on a Saturday?

I picked up the receiver. "Hullo?"

Cecily's voice vibrated with excitement. "I think you were onto something, having me examine this painting more closely. I think you should come take a look."

I shook myself awake, sitting up in bed. "Sure, I'll be there in about forty-five minutes."

Jason looked over. "News?"

I nodded, leaning over to kiss him. "We'll see. That painting might have hidden a secret or two after all." I glanced again at the clock. "Not to worry. I'll be sure to be home by one, so we can leave for the gig."

He smiled. "I'll get everything packed up for us. That way we can head right out when you get here."

It was closer to eleven thirty by the time I pulled into the parking lot before the art museum. Cecily was waiting for me on the front steps, her eyes glowing with energy, and she took me by the arm, half dragging me along with her to her office. When we got there, she directed me over to a large, white table with six lights on swivel mounts stationed on all sides of it. In the center was the painting.

"I started with the top corner," she explained, "I figured if there was nothing to see, that I wouldn't have caused too much damage to it. But as I began to work, I realized you were right. There was something beneath it. It took me all night long, and I've only begun the process, but you can already see what's taking place."

She reached over and flipped a switch on the side of the table. A light glowed from within the table, illuminating the painting from below.

It was as if I was sitting in an optometrist's chair and the doctor had just slid a new lens in on top of an old one. The darker image of the waterfall slid out of focus, and I could see the delicate lines beneath, the brighter colors.

There were the turbaned guests leaning back against the walls, enjoying the wines and spiced meats. The dancing woman on the left smiled with joy. But there were two new characters in this tableau – a couple standing at the center. And I knew in a glance who they were.

My voice was hushed. "Mary painted herself and Xander into the Jewish Wedding."

Cecily's head bobbed with delight. "She did! And look at the fine detail in the faces. The light falling across the scene. It's stunning."

I shook my head. "Why would she have covered it up?"

Cecily shrugged. "You know artists. Always thinking they haven't done it quite to their satisfaction. Or maybe she did this as a practice study, and then was done with that. Maybe she didn't want to be known for derivative works."

She reached over with a finger, tenderly stroking it down the balcony's ridge on the left. "But she was a master, even at her young age. Just look at that. When I finish with the restoration, it will be a treasure."

I smiled. "It's in good hands, then."

* * *

The ride down to Bourne flew by, and in no time at all we were pulling into Meredith's campground. Meredith and her husband Simel were there already, and the exuberant sounds of a soccer game drifted from the TV in their camper. Paul and Adam drove in only minutes later, and soon we were sitting around the picnic table, sharing out slices of pizza and bowls of salad.

There was a movement on the table, and I looked down. I smiled in delight. "What in the world is this thing?"

It looked like a small, brown beetle, about the size of a dime. However, rather than two antennae, it had just one long snout, sort of like a curved, extra-long elephant trunk. Even more intriguing, there were a pair of feathery protuberances from it, about a third of the way down.

Jason glanced over and chuckled. "That's an acorn borer," he explained. "They use that nose to poke a hole into an acorn. They lay their eggs in there, and the young ones grow, safe and sound, surrounded by food."

Paul's eyes sparkled. "All well and good, until the squirrels gather up all the acorns," he pointed out. "Then those eggs might become a tasty treat for the squirrels. Sort of like a chocolate truffle with a soft inside."

Jason took a drink of his Ipswich Ale. "On the other hand, being moved into a squirrel's hoard could be perfect for the baby borers," he pointed out. "They get dropped in an entire room full of delicious food. As long as the squirrels don't get to their particular nut before the borers are big enough, they're all set."

Adam reached for the marshmallows. "I think I'm ready for the s'mores," he said. "Sounds tastier than either acorns or borers to me."

Jason moved around the table. "Let me give you a hand with that fire."

My phone chimed, and I brought it up to see who had emailed me. It was my friend in Germany.

Sorry for the delay. I double-checked just to be sure. No record anywhere of Mary Goldstein from Massachusetts and a grant of any kind. No visa applications, nothing. As far as we can tell, she never intended to set foot in Germany.

Jason looked over from his cross-hatch of sticks. "What is it?"

I shook my head in confusion. "I don't think Mary ever got a grant."

He raised an eyebrow. "You think she turned it down?"

I looked down at the screen. "I think there never even was one," I mused.

He used his lighter to light a corner of the birch bark beneath his grid, and in a moment the fire had flared into life. It licked its way up through the structure, growing in size with each passing second.

Paul grinned. "Now *that's* a fire."

Jason came around to stand beside me. "So why did everyone believe Mary had earned a grant?"

I looked into the fire, into the flickerings of tangerine, crimson, and golden yellow. "I think, tomorrow morning, that I'll ask that very question." I smiled and looked up into his eyes. "But tonight, it's all about the music."

Chapter 25

The sky was cerulean blue, with white clouds drifting across, and I smiled in contentment. Jason looked across the car at me, and his mouth quirked into a grin.

"Not too many people would be that happy, stuck in traffic."

I motioned a hand at the quaint shops around us. "We are in beautiful historic Mystic, Connecticut, and we're waiting for the boat's drawbridge to lower so we can get to the docks. And then we'll spend a delightful afternoon kayaking along the river. What could be better?"

He glanced forward as the convertible black Ferrari before us got impatient with waiting, spun in a tight, growling circle, and raced off in the other direction. "I suppose they were a bit impatient," he commented dryly.

A loud horn blared, and a minute later we were in motion, crossing the bridge and turning right. In short order we were parking in the Noank Shipyard.

We had our kayak activities down to a science, and we were in the river in under fifteen minutes. My eyes lit up in delight as I looked right.

Jason chuckled. "I know, you want to go under the drawbridge."

"Absolutely!"

We paddled our way over, and the cars roared as they drove over our heads. It seemed almost that I could reach up and touch the base of the bridge. I couldn't help myself. I pursed my lips and let out a long "Wooooo!" as I came out the other side of the bridge.

Jason grinned. "Not quite a tunnel," he pointed out.

"Close enough," I countered.

We paddled along the shore of the river, waving to the many people relaxing along the banks. Other kayakers and rowboaters drifted up and down the river. On other kayaking trips we took I sought out trout, egrets, and blue herons. Here it was definitely about the boats and people.

We came up to a gorgeous wooden three-master. I gazed at it, wondering just what it must have been like in the days of the Civil War, heading out onto the open seas in one of these, no GPS systems or radios.

My phone rang.

I laughed out loud, then reached for the dry bag that was clipped by my feet. I set my paddle across my lap as I popped open the seal and withdrew the phone.

I glanced at the screen. "It's Cecily," I called over to Jason.

"About time," he commented. "I think you've left her six messages between yesterday and today."

Cecily sounded sleepy. "Sorry about not getting back to you sooner. I got so absorbed in working on that painting that by the time I got home, I crashed. I think I slept for twelve hours straight. I just saw your messages now."

"I know what that's like," I agreed.

A seagull flew overhead, calling out in joy at the beautiful weather.

Cecily's voice perked up a bit. "What was that?"

"We're kayaking on the Mystic River," I explained. "Just went under the drawbridge."

A thunderous blare shook the water, and I nearly dropped the phone.

Cecily's voice trilled with concern. "What in the world was that?"

Jason pointed, and I grinned. "The drawbridge is going up! We get to watch it from the water!"

I picked up my camera, popped it into video mode, and used my other hand to point it at the bridge. The huge counterweights eased down as the bridge tilted up, slowly, rising to finally point straight up at the sky.

I called into the phone, "Well, I don't have the technology to show you first hand, but I'm taking a video for you. You can watch it tonight on YouTube."

"Very cool," agreed Cecily. "What kinds of boats are coming past?"

"There's a small motorboat and some gorgeous, large sailboats. The last one must be a tour boat of some sort – it's one of those old-style three-masters, like I was just admiring here."

As the larger boat drew near, the group on board burst into song.

"Happy Birthday To You …"

Cecily laughed. "Are they singing Happy Birthday?"

"Yes, indeed, they are. Must be a celebration."

The song finished, and the entire bridge area burst into applause and cheers.

Another blare resounded from the banks, and slowly the bridge creaked its way shut. I waited until the last solid click before ending my recording and putting down the camera.

I smiled as I resumed my conversation with Cecily. "Well, that was exciting. So, now that we're not being recorded any more, did you give it some thought? Who exactly did you hear about Mary's grant from?"

"I am absolutely sure of when I heard the news," responded Cecily. "It was the principal who told me, and he had heard the news from the brothers. Mary herself had never said a word to me about it. Not that she was applying for it, and certainly not that she'd been accepted. It's part of why I was so upset. I thought she had been hiding it from me."

"All right. Thank you, Cecily. If you think of anything else, please let me know."

"I will. And enjoy your kayaking!"

I tucked the phone back into its dry bag, and Jason and I headed back under the bridge. I behaved myself and only let out a quiet "wooo" as we emerged into the light.

We paddled along the right bank of the river, and I looked up into the trees behind a large, brick building. There was a wooden-railed bar tucked amongst the leaves.

I chuckled. "That looks like a treehouse!"

Jason grinned. "Indeed, that's the name of the bar area. I thought we might have dinner there tonight, if you were up for some tuna."

My stomach rumbled at the thought. "Absolutely!"

He nudged his head forward. "But first, there's another treat for you."

I looked ahead. Down past the rows of boats and docks, a large train swing bridge stood in the open position.

My eyes went round. "They have a swing bridge, too? Will we get to see it in motion?"

He looked at me fondly. "Would I deprive you of such a thing?"

If there had been a way for me to pull him into a kiss without sending us both into the river, I would have done it.

Chapter 26

The plumbing shop was closed up when we pulled in front of it, even though it was barely three in the afternoon. Jason glanced at me, and we drove the four minutes down the road to the Milltowne Tavern. A beat-up truck with the brothers' logo was sitting immediately outside. We found a parking spot a few spaces down the road and headed in.

Barry and Ephraim were sitting right where we had left them, looking as if they had not moved an inch in the intervening days. They glanced up as we came in, and deep scowls settled on both of their faces in full stereo.

Jason eased himself to my right, staying between me and the two men. "Mind if we join you?"

Barry harrumphed, but Ephraim shrugged his shoulders in resignation. "Might as well get this over with."

The bartender came by, her dark ponytail swishing. "Two Sams, was it?"

I raised an eyebrow. She was good. Jason nodded and handed over the money when we got our glasses.

Ephraim took a pull of his drink. His voice was surly. "Fine. You know now. Mary never did win any grant."

Jason glanced at me. "Oh?"

Barry leant over. "Don't act all surprised," he challenged. "You got that Cecily woman all worked up, and she called the rabbi. Said she wanted to know if he had heard anything about the details. Next thing we know, he's showing up at our office this morning. And ... well ..."

Ephraim's face tinted. "You can't lie to a rabbi," he explained. "We had to come clean."

I tried to keep my tone encouraging. "Of course you did. And it was so long ago."

Ephraim snorted. "Yeah, back when I was engaged to Rachel. Back when she was firm and trim. Not like the fat slob she became once we were married." He nudged his head. "And Barry here was courting Miss Estelle."

Barry's eyes lit up. "Man, you should have seen her. She could have been a Jewish Lauren Bacall."

The corner of my mouth quirked up. "Lauren Bacall *was* Jewish," I pointed out.

"Well, then, there you go," he stated, as if that explained everything. "Sultry lips, sexy body, what more could you want from a woman?"

He looked down into his drink. "But women are all the same. They only care about a man's wallet. They get antsy at any sign that the guy can't take care of his family."

A glimmer shone in my mind. "So when Mary disappeared, you figured she ran off? And you didn't want Miss Estelle to find out about that?"

He nodded morosely. "How would that look? Here I'm trying to prove to this sex goddess that I'm the man for her, that I can take care of everything. And I can't even take care of some kid sister? Who's scampering around with some gentile caddy?"

He shook his head. "Mary was gone a week. No sign of coming back. And Miss Estelle comes over for drinks. What am I going to say? My sister has joined the circus?" He scoffed. "I figured, what's the harm. The git has gone, without a backward glance. Not even a note for us. We deserved to have some joy in our lives, after all we sacrificed for her. And if she did come back, we could just say that she turned down the grant. That she decided to stay with her family."

Ephraim leant over. "As she should have," he growled.

My eyes shadowed. "Someone killed her," I pointed out.

Barry downed his drink. "If she'd stayed home, like she was supposed to, that never would have happened," he returned. "We kept her safe. We took her from home to school and school to home. No harm ever came to her then. It was only when she got in with ..." He waved a hand in the air. "Those other sorts, that all the trouble began. Staying out late. Going strange places. We told her not to, and she ignored us." His fingers turned white on the glass. "And look what ended up happening."

Barry waved over the bartender, who promptly brought him a fresh glass. He looked into it. "Didn't even matter, in the end, our story about the grant," he muttered. "Miss Estelle met a throat surgeon at some Bar Mitzvah, and next thing I know, she's engaged to him. Gold digging bimbo."

Ephraim nudged him. "Yeah, but remember when we saw her last year in the supermarket?"

Barry's eyes lit up. "Right, talk about a whale! I would've needed a harpoon for that one."

Jason glanced at me.

I nodded. "Thank you so much for your time, and I'm so sorry for your loss."

Ephraim gave a half wave. "Right, right."

By the time we reached the main entrance and looked back, the two men were nearly lost in the shadows.

Chapter 27

The torrential rainstorms of last night had long since stopped, leaving the back porch glistening in the late morning sunlight. I stepped over to the side railing, looking along the slope to where it came up to the end post. This was where the little grey tree frog had rested for the past week, serenely watching over my yoga stance.

He was gone.

Jason poked his head out the back slider. He took in the consternation on my face and stepped out to join me. "He's not there?"

I shook my head, carefully stepping around the porch, watching where my feet landed. Jason moved down the steps to the grass and circled from the outside.

At last I sighed and rolled out my mat. "Maybe the soft mud was ideal for him to build a burrow in," I surmised. "Maybe he's preparing his fall nest."

He smiled at that. "Could be. Autumn is coming, after all."

A delicate brown dragonfly settled onto one of our jalapeño plants, and Jason chuckled. "Speaking of which, here comes our first autumn meadowhawk. Right on time."

I looked over to the hummingbird feeder, where a pair of rufous were engaging in an aerial dogfight for possession of the nectar. "And soon the hummingbirds will head south. The cycles keep moving around."

He came over to kiss me on my forehead. "Namaste, darling." He headed back inside, and I was left with the gentle clouds, the soft breezes, and the serenely blinking eyes of the delicate dragonfly.

* * *

We pulled into the parking space at the Singletary boat ramp, and it felt odd not to have the kayaks on the roof. Jason had some work to do further north, and my own backlog had stacked up, so we had to keep the visit quick. Still, I wanted to talk to Xander in person.

There was a middle-aged woman sitting next to him on the dock, their rods dangling into the water side by side, and it wasn't until we had come up to them that I recognized her.

"Cheryl!"

She turned and smiled. "Morgan, nice to see you." She lifted up her six-pack of Diet Sprite. "Want something to drink?"

I shook my head. "Catching anything?"

Xander's face looked gentler than the last times I'd seen him, with more color in his cheeks. His eyes had lost their sunken look. "A few, but we sent them back," he explained. "It's too nice a day to keep any. They are enjoying life, just as we are."

Cheryl rested her rod across her knees. "How can we help you? Seems you're not here to kayak today."

I looked to Xander. "I can come back another time if –"

He waved off my concern. "I've told Cheryl everything. Told the entire AA group. It was a load off my chest, to talk about it. If you still have questions, feel free to ask them. I'll answer what I can."

I flushed, but nodded and pressed on. "Were you and Mary planning on running off together?"

He gave a wry smile. "If she'd have gone with me, I would have left in a heartbeat. To Miami, to Dallas, to wherever she wanted to go. We could have had a fresh start together."

I raised an eyebrow. "But she had two years of high school left. And you were planning on going to Tufts."

His look shadowed. "I would have given it all up for her. Those others were no good for her. Cecily was almost her pimp by that point, pushing her to perform, driving her to paint faster. Cecily was going to write a book about Mary and was going to grow famous on her coattails."

"Didn't Mary's brothers protect her?"

He shook his head. "Those two were just as bad. They still treated her like she was six years old. Wanted her straight home from school, wanted her to be an automaton of perfection." A gleam came to his eye. "But Mary was finding her inner strength. I think talking with all of the families of the Holocaust victims helped with that. I think she realized, with all these others had gone through, that her own hurdles were tiny in comparison. By the time that summer came around, she was challenging her brothers."

"Oh?"

He nodded. "I know I was tough on my parents during my teenage years, but it was like a fire had been ignited within her, and she was determined not to let it go out. It seemed every time I visited that there was a shouting match of some kind going on."

I glanced at Jason. "Dogs and cats living together, mass hysteria."

Xander scrunched his brow. "Huh?"

I smiled. "A line from *Ghostbusters*. Always seems to come to mind in situations like you described."

He shrugged. "Oh, I never got to see that one. In any case, despite her flares of rebellion, Mary was still a traditionalist. She chafed at the rules, but she wanted to finish high school with her friends. She was planning to attend the Massachusetts College of Art and Design, in Boston."

He looked out at the glistening water. "It wasn't just the schooling. She wanted to attend the same temple she'd been at as a child. To be near her brothers and keep an eye on them. To keep working with her mentor and further hone her skills." He gave a wry smile. "As much as she would complain and vent, she loved her community. I don't think she ever would have left it."

I looked down at him, my voice somber. "So, who could she have been at that drive-in with?"

His eyes shadowed. "I've been thinking about that since her body was identified. I honestly don't know. I thought things were fine between us that summer. She'd injured her arm, and was spending time on various projects, so when I didn't hear from her for a few days, I didn't think anything of it. And when I finally reached her brothers and they said she'd left for Germany …" He looked down. "I thought she had abandoned me. Left without a word. I was broken. I lost all sense of the world."

Cheryl twined her fingers into his. "And now you are getting it back again."

He looked up, light returning to his eyes. "Yes."

Jason looked between them. "So she just disappears. The brothers think she's with you, you think she's with the art teacher, and nobody quite has a handle on her. She goes into that drive-in and she never comes out."

I looked over to Jason. "Maybe I can dig up the drive-in schedule from old archives of the Telegram. We know when she broke her arm, and we know from the hospital records that she had follow-up visits for three weeks after that. Maybe that might help."

Xander nodded. "It's something about that drive-in," he agreed. "She and I went to every movie there. I just can't see her going with someone else."

"I'll keep digging," I promised. "I will push and pull, and something will emerge."

His look shadowed, and he took a deep breath. Then he looked up at me. "I've been avoiding the drive-in – but I think it might be time. Would you go there with me tomorrow?"

Jason's eyes flashed with worry, and he gave a small shake of his head.

Cheryl leant over. "Xander, dear, you have that job interview tomorrow, remember? At Blackstone National?"

He blinked. "Oh, of course. Yes." He looked up at me. "Thursday, then?"

Jason's brow eased slightly, and he put his hand on my shoulder. "I'm free on Thursday," he agreed. "Maybe about five?"

Xander seemed to hesitate, but then he nodded. "Five it is."

I looked out at the water. "In the meantime, best of luck with your fishing."

As we walked back to our car, I saw Cheryl wrap an arm around his waist, giving him a tender hug.

Jason pulled us out of the parking lot. He looked over to me. "What do you think?"

I shook my head. "It all comes down to that drive-in," I mused. "Over a quarter of a century ago, and it comes down to who she drove through that stone arch with. Whoever it was took her in and never brought her back out."

Chapter 28

Jason's kayak drifted to my right, and I breathed in a lungful of the early afternoon breeze. The clouds above reflected perfectly in the still surface of the aptly named Stump Pond in Westborough. Only three other kayaks were out in the water. Along with the great blue heron, turtles, and countless, friendly dragonflies, there were a stunning number of swans congregating. I was sure there were over fifty of their sturdy white bodies at the far end of the water.

I glanced at Jason. "I always thought swans were territorial. Do you think they're getting ready to migrate south?"

"Mute swans were brought in from Europe, and they don't have any set migration patterns here in the US," mused Jason, staying between me and the horde. "They do sometimes move based on weather. It could be they're preparing to head south-ish as it starts to get chilly. Still, there's a pair of swans that stays at a pond in Rhode Island all winter long, even when the surface is mostly ice."

I eyed the thick wings of one of the swans as it stretched. "Well, I wouldn't want to rile that pack up."

He nodded. "We definitely want to keep our distance. One or two swans could be trouble enough. With that many, I wouldn't want to count the odds."

A dragonfly flitted past my head, and in a moment I could see tiny feet curling around the edge of the brim of my hat. "I seem to have a passenger."

He grinned. "Indeed you do. Just watch out for those stumps, lest you both end up wetter than you'd like."

Stump Pond, technically known as Mill Pond, was formed in 1968 when Westborough flooded a forest area to make a reservoir. However, unlike most similar floodings, in this case they decided to leave all the trees in place. Over the decades the trees had collapsed, falling in, but the trunks still remained, just below the water's surface. I had gotten stuck on one more times than I could count, but Jason always patiently hauled me back off them again.

My phone rang within its dry bag, and I chuckled. I slid the button through the case and called in, "Can you hear me?"

A muffled voice replied. "Yes, barely."

"Hold on," I instructed. "I need to get the phone out."

I balanced my paddle across my legs and turned the two plastic latches that held the bag sealed shut. In a moment I had the phone to my ear. "Hello, I've got you now. We're out kayaking."

"Oh, how nice," came the woman's voice. "It's Cecily."

"Hey there, Cecily." Jason had pulled close to me and nodded at the name. I drew my eyes out to the swans. "How can I help you?"

"I'll be brief, so you can get back to your kayaking. I was wondering if we could meet later this evening."

"Sure thing. At the Art Museum?"

"No, I was thinking … could we meet at the Singing Falls, on the Blackstone River?"

"That's fine, what time?"

"How about six?"

"Sure, I'll be there. See you at six."

I tucked the phone back into its bag, sealing it in, and took up my paddle.

Jason looked over at me. "I thought the art museum closed at five?"

I nodded. "She wants to meet me over at the waterfall on Blackstone Street, just off of 122A. The place Mary painted that image of."

His gaze shadowed. "Morgan, I have that event I need to manage. It's why I didn't want you going off with Xander alone to the drive-in today."

I gave him a reassuring smile. "Well, but this is Cecily," I soothed him. "The worst she wields is a painter's brush. And besides, Tricentennial Park at Singing Falls is the size of a postage stamp. Blackstone Street curves right around the park and over the river. We'll be in full sight the entire time."

His lips drew into a thin line. "That road is barely traveled," he pointed out. "You could be there twenty minutes and not see a single car."

"I'll keep my phone on me, I promise. And I'll check in regularly."

He reached out a hand, and I took it in mine. His gaze was steady on me. "If you were to vanish, I wouldn't take a relative's word for where you'd gone," he murmured. "I would want to make certain that you were all right. That, for whatever reason you left, you were happy where you'd gone."

I gave his fingers a squeeze. "If I ever do vanish, come after me." My voice went hoarse. "For I would never voluntarily leave your side. If I was gone, it would be against my will, and I would be doing everything in my power to return to you."

His gaze deepened, and there was no need for words.

* * *

A shiver of trepidation ran down my spine as I stared at the rumbling waterfall from the small overlook. Jason was right. While the narrow road was only a few feet from me, I had not seen a single car on it since my arrival ten minutes ago. Cecily was apparently running late. I wore a light windbreaker and the phone was in my jacket, Jason's icon an easy finger-press away. I'd already touched base with him twice.

There was a rumble of tires, and I turned to see a crimson Prius pull into the parking lot, Cecily behind the wheel. I tapped the phone and put it to my ear. Jason answered on the first ring.

"She's here," I reported. "I'll call you as soon as we're through."

"I'll be watching my phone." His voice was tense. "Call if anything feels off."

"Don't worry, I will."

I tucked the phone in my pocket as Cecily climbed out of the car. She pulled a wide tote bag from the seat next to her, then came down the path to join me. Her face seemed quiet.

I nodded as she came to a stop next to me. "Greetings, Cecily."

She nodded in return, then turned to look down at the rolling water. The waterfall wasn't huge, perhaps ten feet high by thirty feet wide, but with the road going over the river just past it the sound was magnified by the metal and concrete.

I leaned against the railing again, admiring the drifting clouds. Apparently Cecily needed to take her time with this, and I had no objection to letting her proceed when she was ready.

At last she sighed and looked down at the bag. "Madeline thought you should have this."

I raised an eyebrow. "Madeline?"

She nodded. "My wife. And I ..." She sighed, her shoulders slumping. "I know she's right. Mary would have wanted you to have it."

I knelt by the bag and opened it up. I drew out the painting within, holding it up in the light.

Cecily had done a stunning job of restoring it. Gone were any remnants of the scene before us. The darker blues and greys had been completely rinsed away. What remained was the vibrant red-orange of the guitar player's shirt, the joy on the bride's face, and the contentment in the groom's. The Jewish wedding had been brought to fresh life, with the happy couple as its centerpiece.

I looked up at Cecily. "Are you sure? Mary gave this to you."

Cecily shook her head. "I think Mary was only keeping it from harm. She did not want it in her house. But I had a sense that she would want it back, once she was through with college and starting her own life." She looked down at the shimmering waters. "She never quite made it that far."

I gazed at the happy couple, at the hope they had for their future. When I spoke, my voice was hoarse.

"Would it be all right to you if I passed it along to another?"

She looked up at that. "But you're the one who found her. You're the one who let her rest easy."

I met her eyes. "There were more than three lives impacted by her vanishing."

Her brow creased. "Xander is a drunken troublemaker. Are you sure he would even appreciate it?"

I gave a soft smile. "I could at least ask him. And I think he is getting his steps into more of a straight line now. It's just taken him a little while."

Her gaze shadowed, and at last she nodded. "It is yours, to do with as you wish," she agreed. "If you want to talk with Xander about it, then that is your choice."

Her lips pressed together. "Although, you know –"

There was the rumble of a car engine, and a Sutton police car crawled its way down from the north, easing its way across the bridge. A fond warmth eased through me. Jason might not have been able to be here in person, but he would apparently not have me unguarded.

Cecily watched the patrol car finish its half loop around us and head on toward 122A. She let out a breath. "I suppose I was just jealous of Xander," she muttered. "Mary had such amazing talent. A gift that many would give everything they had for. And she wasted so much of her time going to movies with him, going walking with him. I still remember when she broke her arm at that godforsaken riding party. She could have permanently destroyed her ability to paint! And all for a *boy*." She sighed, shaking her head. "I resented him. I resented every moment he took her away from me." Her gaze became lost in the grey bumbling of water and air. "And then she was gone forever."

She gave herself a shake, then turned. Her voice regained its tone. "In any case, the painting is yours, and I have handed the last of mine over to the auction house."

"You didn't keep one for yourself?"

"Just one. A small portrait of me she did, when she and I first met." She gave a half smile. "It reminds me of her in her earliest stages. Fresh. Young. Unworried. That's the way I'd like to remember her."

She nodded, then turned. She strode off to her Prius, slid in, and in a moment she was heading out of the parking lot.

I drew the cell from my pocket and pushed the icon. In a moment Jason was there. "Everything all right?"

"Everything is fine," I agreed. "She's left. And thank you for the patrol car."

I heard the smile in his voice. "Just keeping an eye on things," he agreed. "What did she want?"

I looked down at the painting. "She wanted to give us Mary's painting of the Jewish Wedding."

I could hear his surprised intake of air. "Isn't that going to be worth a fair amount?"

I ran a hand along the frame. "I wasn't thinking of keeping it – or selling it."

There was a pause, and when he spoke, his voice was warm. "I think you are wise and wonderful."

I smiled. I tucked the painting back into its bag and made my way back to my car. "I'm heading home," I let him know. "Get back to your event, and then come home to me."

"Always."

Chapter 29

Rush hour traffic was in full gridlock on 146 as we pulled to a stop in front of the drive-in entrance. The stone arch seemed even more precarious than before, and I slung the tote bag over one arm before scurrying beneath it. Jason moved easily at my side, his eyes scanning the weed-strewn, undulating pavement. "No car parked out front."

I checked my watch. "Ten of five," I reported. "He's still got time."

Jason stayed at my side, carefully surveying the birch and pine at the edge of the clearing. "Or he could be here already."

I bit my lip, turning to examine the large, dilapidated screen which stretched across the front of the open field. I felt Xander was innocent of what had happened, but I'd been wrong in the past. Better to let Jason stay alert, just in case.

There was a rumble of tire on pavement; Jason's shoulders eased as a dilapidated car pulled in behind ours. Xander climbed out, giving the door a solid slam to ensure it latched. Then he slowly trudged through the gate and up the grass-speckled path. His eyes were down on the ground before him.

He didn't come straight to us. Instead he veered away from the screen, navigated up three ridges of the rippled blacktop, and moved in to a location immediately before the projection house. Then he turned and stared at the screen. I could see now that tears were streaming down from his eyes.

I walked toward him. "Xander – I'm so sorry."

He shook his head, making no move to wipe his face. "This was our spot," he explained. "Right here. It's where we always parked. From when I first met her, we spent every chance we could here. It was our one way to get away from all the watching eyes – to be truly alone. We would nestle up here in a blanket, with a bucket of popcorn and a soda to share, and the world would fall away." His eyes were locked on the patchwork of grey and ivory which now made up the screen. "And it's all gone. It's all fallen apart."

I ran a hand through my hair. "I looked up the movies they were playing that night. It was *Ghostbusters* and *Gremlins*. Does that strike any chord? Any memory at all?"

He shook his head. "I never saw either of those. Maybe she would have gone with a girlfriend – but why wouldn't that girl have reported her missing? If she'd gone alone, the police would have found a car here. It just doesn't make any sense."

He knelt to the ground, running his fingers through the grass. "She stepped here," he mused. "Her feet touched this soil."

He dropped into silence.

I glanced at Jason, then back down at Xander. "I'm not sure if you're up to it … but would you want to see where she was found?"

He looked up at me in confusion. "Found?"

I flushed. "Her … her body."

He drew to his feet, blinking. "Oh, yes, of course." He shook his head. "For so many years I've thought of this very spot here as 'our location.' When I heard she was found at the drive-in, I simply imagined this place, here." He ran a hand through his hair. "But of course she wasn't found in this spot. She must have been somewhere else." He turned and looked toward the back of the clearing, past the projection booth. His face shadowed. "I would imagine back there somewhere?"

I shook my head. "Actually, she was found to the right of the screen, about a hundred yards in."

His brow scrunched in confusion, but he nodded. "Yes, I would like to see it."

I guided us forward, toward the screen. "There's an easier way in from the front edge of the land, up here. That's the way the police and other personnel came in and out. Coming in from the side of the drive-in area, the way Jason and I originally went, there's a number of ravines and such to contend with."

He followed dutifully behind without comment.

We made our way down to the open area on the other side of the screen, then followed the beaten brush path made by the various crews. It was only a few minutes before the white bark of the birch trees shone out, and we came up to the area. The police tape and other markers were long gone, but the dug-up earth and gaping hole remained as a ragged testament to the lost life.

Xander groaned in agony, then dropped to both knees, digging his hands into the soft dirt. He bent his head and his shoulders shook. I laced my fingers into Jason's, remaining quiet. I could not imagine what Xander must be going through. All those years he had probably railed against Mary, been furious with her for so callously abandoning him. And all that time she had been an innocent victim, curled up in the deep moss, patiently waiting for justice.

At long last Xander's sobbing eased. He drew an arm across his eyes. Then his hand went to his back pocket, he pulled out the black handle of a fishing knife, and with the flick of his wrist he popped it open.

Jason was in front of me before I could breathe, dropping down into a crouch, easing onto the balls of his feet.

Xander stared at his knife for a moment, then rose to his feet.

Jason's voice was a low thrum of warning. "Xander, you don't want to –"

Xander turned as if he hadn't heard Jason, then took the few steps to the nearest birch tree. It was large and stately, with a trunk at least six inches in circumference. Xander looked at it for a moment, and then started carving. He began at the top, making a high, rounded arc, then drew diagonally down to a point. Reversing the process, he finished his heart. Then he focused in for the names.

I could see the shimmer of relief in Jason's stance, but he did not move, staying resolutely between me and Xander.

At last Xander had finished his work and stepped back from the tree. He flipped the blade back into its case and returned it to his pocket.

His voice was a whisper. "There, my love. I should have known you wouldn't just give up on us. I should have trusted in you."

I looked down at the tote bag, then stepped to the left, to draw alongside Jason. I held the bag forward.

"Here, Xander. I think you should have this."

It took him a moment to draw his eyes away from the carven heart, and his brow creased in confusion when he saw the bag. He shrugged and took it from me, placing it at his feet.

He drew out the painting ... and stopped.

Fresh tears blossomed in his eyes, but this time his face glowed with surprise and gratitude. "She ... she painted this?"

I nodded. "She painted it, and then she painted over it with a scene of the Blackstone Waterfall. It was a secret. She gave it to Cecily for safe keeping, but Cecily had no idea what its significance was." My throat grew tight. "I think it was Mary's ... Mary's way of preserving hope. Of knowing that, if she set it down in paint, eventually it would come true."

He nodded, his eyes soaking in the scene. "She loved that painting at the art museum," he murmured. "She would sit and stare at it for the longest time."

He gave a smile of almost child-like joy. "She has given me an image," he sighed. "Just like she would do for the other families who were left behind. I have one of my own now. Something to remember her by. Something to celebrate the joy we shared. To focus on the good times."

He reverentially put the painting back into the bag, then stepped toward me, drawing me into a warm hug. He held me for several long moments before releasing me. Then he turned and did the same with Jason.

His voice was hoarse when he spoke. "Thank you. Thank you both."

His phone rang, and he glanced down at his hip. "Excuse me a moment." He brought the phone to his ear. "Yeah? Oh, Derrick. No, I'm at the drive-in. The Olive Garden? Sure, yeah. Probably ten minutes."

He hung up and looked at us. "Derrick wants to take me to dinner. His house is being worked on, or something, and I think he wants to repair our friendship as well." He gave a soft smile. "I guess I do, too. Things are seeming clearer again for me, clearer than they've been in a long time."

I nodded, and we guided him back out of the forest, around behind the large, dilapidated screen and through the tumbling down stone arch. When we got to the cars, he shook both of our hands. Then he climbed in his dilapidated car and rattled away.

Jason slipped an arm around my waist. "Well, at least some good has come of all of this."

I sighed, leaning up against him. "That new show, *Cold Justice*, starts up in a few days, and its promos claim there are over 200,000 unsolved murder cases on the books. And that's just cases they have records for." I looked back to the drive-in, the pavement and large screen crumbling in on itself. "Maybe it was wishful thinking that we could do any better for Mary. She's been dead nearly thirty years. There's barely any evidence. Maybe the best we can do is bring closure for those who loved her."

He pressed his lips to my forehead. "Then that will be enough."

Chapter 30

The images before me were haunting. A group of women held their hands out, mourning, pleading, while chaos rained down on all sides. I had come back to the Worcester Art Museum to take a look at an exhibition I'd missed on my previous visits – *Cri du Couer* by Nancy Spero.

On first glance it was a simple enough presentation. The room was completely empty except for a foot-high border running around the bottom of the wall. You started at the right, and initially the figures seemed content, perhaps making the usual prayers for good health and long life. But soon the danger became palpable. Dark storm clouds roiled around them. The figures' faces could barely be seen. Their organized prayers turned into undulating chaos. And then, finally, they were lost in the storm. There was panel after panel of dark, tumultuous clouds and death.

My phone rang.

There was nobody else in the gallery except a bored guard, but even so I flushed with embarrassment and strode out the door into the main hallway. I tucked myself in an alcove by the elevator and hit the answer button. "Yes?"

The voice on the other end seethed with fury. "You took Xander to see Mary?!?"

I blinked in surprise. "Barry?"

"Hell yes, it's Barry," he shouted, "and you had no right!"

"I'm sorry, I had no idea you'd be so upset," I stammered.

"Ephraim and I are driving over to the drive-in right now. I want you to meet us there, so you can tell us exactly what that bastard said to you."

My stomach twisted in confusion and guilt. "Said to me?"

"I never did trust him as far as I could throw him," he snapped. "We'll be there in fifteen minutes." The phone went dead.

I punched the icon for Jason. He picked up after a ring. His voice was cool and refreshing, like a tall glass of iced tea after a scorching day in the sun. "Hey there, sweetie."

"Tell me you're free and you're near Sutton."

His tone snapped to a serious tenor. "What's wrong?"

"I've upset Mary's brothers. They're furious with me for talking to Xander. They seem to think he's guilty of something. They want me to meet them at the drive-in and show them exactly what happened yesterday."

"I'm about twenty minutes away," he stated. "I'm leaving now. Do *not* go into that complex without me."

"I won't – I promise."

"OK. I'm heading out. See you soon."

Again I was left with a silent phone in my hand.

I tucked it into my purse and hurried down the stairs to my car. My heart thundered against my chest. What in the world had I done wrong? Xander's request had seemed innocent enough – but had I missed something?

In a moment I was hopping on 290, taking the exit for 146 South, and streaking along past where the Honey Dew Donuts used to be, before the arrival of jersey barriers had put them out of business. The sky was right out of Maxfield Parrish's *Ecstasy* painting, with stunning blue and white, fluffy clouds, but I felt none of the joy the girl in that image shone with. Rather, I would have dove off that cliff, hoping for deep, opaque waters to swim through, to hide beneath until the storms passed.

There – the drive-in was up ahead, and I saw that there was now a chain hanging across the entrance, gilded with yellow plastic. There was also a large log in place, presumably to prevent cars from driving in and causing trouble. Along the front of the area was parked a Confederate grey van with white lettering on it.

I pulled up behind it, leaving myself enough space to easily pull out again. I put the car into park, then sat there for a moment, eyeing my phone, my heart still tripping along at a fast pace.

There was movement. Both doors ahead of me swung open. Barry and Ephraim emerged from the van, their bodies moving ponderously and deliberately, like battleships on the prowl. The two men slowly turned.

I put my hand down on the shifter.

There was the sound of fast tires behind me, and Jason's truck raced in immediately behind mine, slamming on the brakes to tuck to a stop inches from my bumper. He was out of his car before the dust finished its billow, coming up to stand alongside my door.

His eyes were steady on the two approaching men. His voice was calm, but held an edge to it. "What's this all about?"

Barry's face glowed crimson. "She let that bastard in," he snarled. "She took *him* to see Mary's resting place!"

Jason's voice remained cool. "Mary is in the Sutton cemetery, buried with honors," he pointed out. "She is at peace."

"No thanks to *him*," snapped Barry. "He should have never been allowed anywhere near her!"

Jason held his gaze. "Just how did you hear about our meeting yesterday?"

Barry pulled up, his eyes flashing. "Why the hell does that matter?"

Ephraim came up alongside his brother. His brow held deep wrinkles, but he seemed calmer than Barry. "We were doing work on Derrick's new bathroom," he explained. "Derrick called Xander when he was out here with you."

Barry turned and strode to the gate, tucking under the yellow cable. "I want to hear everything he said to you. From the beginning."

Ephraim looked at us, shrugging. "He gets this way sometimes. Especially about Xander. Best thing is to humor him. It'll all blow over, once he realizes it was innocent."

Jason's brow was creased, but he drew open my car door, helping me to stand. We moved along with Ephraim, following after Barry, who was storming ahead as if he was preparing to take Normandy Beach.

Barry's voice echoed across the empty clearing. "So you arrived first? And he came to you? Where did you go?"

I gestured ahead. "To about half-way between the front row and the projection booth," I indicated. "He said that was their favorite place to park."

Barry whirled on Ephraim. "And you called me paranoid! I told you they were sneaking out together. All those times Mary claimed she was studying with Judy, and they were here, fornicating!"

Ephraim made a soothing gesture with his hands. "I'm sure they were just watching the movie, Barry. They weren't up in the back row of some dingy theater. They were right in the middle of all the families, the little kids."

Barry harrumphed, but his color eased. His voice lost some of its snap. "How many times did they come here? Once? Twice?"

I reddened. I felt guilty about sharing Xander's past, but maybe this would help Barry and Ephraim find some closure, to have a better sense of what Mary's final months were like. "I think it was more than that," I admitted. "But Ephraim is right. Xander said they would just eat popcorn together. They were simply enjoying some quiet time – time away from the pressures of school and her projects."

Barry's lips thinned. "Quiet time," he growled. "They could have had that on the couch in our living room, drinking tea and eating Lorna Doone cookies. She didn't have to lie to us."

Ephraim ran a hand through his hair. "If she wanted to see a movie, she did," he pointed out. "We never would have let her go."

Barry snorted. "Of course not. We know what men are like. Xander only wanted one thing from her."

I shook my head. "I didn't get that sense from Xander at all," I countered. "He treated her with respect. I believe he honestly loved Mary."

Barry laughed. "Love? What does a teenaged boy know about love? The only thing he cares about is getting a girl to give in. Then he moves on to the next one."

Jason's voice was calm. "Not all boys – or men – are like that."

Barry smirked. "Of course you would say that – your woman is standing right there next to you."

Jason stilled, but he was silent.

Barry looked around, drawing his eyes from the crack-lines on the large screen to the abandoned piles of thread-bare tires. "OK, so then what? He insisted on going to her burial place?"

I glanced to the woods. "Actually, I'm the one who –"

Barry had already turned and was striding straight to the treeline. "I'm sure he let you believe that," he snapped. "But Xander is a master manipulator. Always was. He sets his sights on something and his devious mind works out any number of angles to achieve his goal. He's like a spider, sitting in the center of a web, and no matter where you turn – there he is."

He plowed through the Virginia creeper, and we followed behind, taking a small hop over a ravine, curling right after him when he came to a large outcropping of granite. We moved between a pair of elderly oaks, then up a small rise.

I glanced left, to where I knew the larger path was, the one the police and investigators had been using. "Maybe if we could just –"

"It's just ahead," he grumbled, pushing past a wild strawberry plant. "Around this corner."

We moved alongside a stump blossoming with turkey tail mushroom, and there it was. The small clearing, the open grave, the small stand of birch.

Barry's grimace eased as we stepped into the sunlight. "Thank God. It doesn't seem like he's –"

His eyes swung to the larger birch before us, and his gaze widened in unbelieving fury. "What in the world has he done?"

Jason eased in front of me. "He only thought –"

Barry's shriek could be heard full back to 146. *"He has desecrated Mary's shrine!"*

Ephraim came up alongside him. "Barry, it's all right. It's only a –"

Barry rounded on him, his face mottled in fury. "That's what you always say! You always say it's all right. It will be OK. And then look at what happens! She's dead! It's all Xander's fault!" His eyes became steely. "And he is going to pay."

Ephraim put a hand on Barry's arm. "Barry, I think we should –"

Barry's hand flew to his hip pocket, and it came out with a folded, black-handled knife, which he whipped open with an easy movement. "I've had enough of your thoughts," he snarled. He spun to the tree and hacked at it, gouging out the heart, obliterating the names with harsh, heavy strokes. Sweat shone on his forehead when he finished and looked back to his brother. "Next comes that boy. It's time to end this once and for all."

Ephraim shook his head. "Not this time, Barry. Not Xander. He's a good kid."

Barry's eyes glowed with heat. "That bastard killed our Mary," he snapped.

Ephraim remained in front of him. "No, he didn't," he stated, his voice hollow. "Xander was innocent."

Barry took a step forward, glaring up at his brother. "He was not! It was all his fault! And anyone who says otherwise is –"

Ephraim blew out his breath. "I say otherwise."

Barry's voice rose to a high squeak. "What?"

Ephraim held his gaze. "Barry, I'm bone tired. I'm fifty-five years old. I'm divorced. What do I have to show for my life?" His gaze gentled. "Mary's dead, Barry. She's dead. And if we could just –"

"Stop right there!" shrieked Barry. "You stop right there, or I'll –"

Ephraim turned to me and Jason. "It's time the truth came out. Long past time. Because Mary loved Xander and was planning –"

"Stop!" screamed Barry, diving forward.

There was a long, shuddering groan as his blade dug deep into Ephraim's abdomen.

For a long moment the world hung, stationary, and dust motes shimmered in the afternoon sun. Then Barry withdrew the blade. Ephraim slowly, soundlessly slithered to the ground.

Barry stared at his brother for a long moment, not speaking, his shoulders solidifying to stone. Then, with the slow deliberation of a Mark 7 heavy gun rotating in its turret to face an enemy, he turned to face me and Jason.

His eyes glittered. A single drop of crimson blood fell from the edge of his knife.

Jason dropped into a crouch. His voice held the sharpness of a command.

"Morgan, run!"

I dropped my purse and lit out, faster than a panicked jackrabbit, quicker than a racing cheetah. I had no idea what direction I was going in. All I knew was I had to get help before things got any worse.

I clambered over boulders, ducked under thick branches, and the only sound in the world was the heavy pounding of my blood in my ears.

The world streamed … streamed …

A heavy root caught my foot. I splayed full force on my face, the impact stunning me.

There was no sound of pursuit. After a moment I realized, perhaps more importantly, that there was no sound of the traffic from 146. Somehow I must have run in the wrong direction. I reached down for my phone – and realized I had left that back in the clearing when I had fled.

I drew to my feet. My right ankle throbbed, and I balanced on my left. I looked around me, my body shaking in time with my heartbeats. I had to go back. If I got further lost, Jason could die before I finally made my way out. At least if I was there, I could help somehow.

I could barely breathe, my throat was so tight, as I cautiously, painstakingly crept back in the direction I'd come in. I came up over a ridge and stopped. There - I could hear grunts and groans of men locked in a struggle. My heart pounded in fear, but I pushed forward. Another ravine, another patch of dense pricker bush. The noises grew louder.

Then, at last, a final outcropping of granite. I rounded it. Ahead, through the dense network of trees, was the birch clearing.

Jason had peeled off his jacket and wrapped it around his left arm, creating a protective shield. He held a thick stick in the other hand. Barry lunged at him, stabbing high, and Jason swept with the stick, deflecting the blow.

Jason's voice held calm. "Give yourself up, Barry," he urged. "Tell your side of the story. I'm sure they'll understand."

Barry's response was high and sharp. "Never! Most juries are run by women. How could you ever trust a woman to think logically! They could never understand why I had to do what I did."

There was a motion behind him. Ephraim was staggering up to one knee, his stomach drenched in blood, his eyes pleading. "Barry – let it go. I can't lose you as well. Give yourself up. Let's take responsibility for what we've done."

Barry's eyes never left Jason's. "Just one good slash and it'll all be over," he muttered. "The threat will be gone. Everything will be all right."

Ephraim groaned and climbed to his feet. "Barry, you're all I have left."

Barry didn't turn. "Then help me, God damn you!"

Jason's gaze swept between the two men, every muscle in his body in sharp tension, as he waited … waited …

Ephraim lunged.

Jason leapt back, but it was not toward him that Ephraim's body flew. Instead, Ephraim dove toward his brother, letting out a low cry.

Barry spun, his knife-hand flashing, and the blade drove deep into Ephraim's side.

Jason lunged forward, wrapping his arms around Barry's body, looking to pin his arms to his side. The three of them strained, flailed, as if they were one large organism, a Hindu god of destruction, six arms locked in battle.

Barry bellowed in fury, he whipped around in a circle, and both Jason and Barry fell back into the dense leaves, crimson drenching their fronts.

My world crashed to a halt. A ragged scream of agony echoed through the clearing; it was a moment before I realized it had been ripped from my own soul.

Barry looked up straight at me, his eyes gleaming, and then he was crashing toward me through the underbrush.

I spun and fled in an absolute panic. My fingers shredded as I clambered over granite outcroppings, my hair pulled as I dove through thick branches, but none of it registered more than a fleeting thought. A large ravine opened up before me, and I vaulted it, scrambling up the other side. A pricker bush slashed at my face, but I plowed on, every ounce of my body shouting to *run, run, run*.

A hand grabbed at the flowing banner of my hair, and I screamed. He yanked, and I was flung face-down into dense moss.

I rolled hard to the right, and he swung with his free hand, smashing his fist against the side of my head. I coughed out a low groan, shaking my head to fend off waves of nausea. I scrabbled back, but he landed astride of me, pinning me at my waist with his heavy weight. My legs were trapped, and he pressed his left hand on my shoulder, holding me down. His right hand held the knife. The blade glittered in the light, a sheen of crimson glimmering along its length.

Jason's blood.

My eyes filled with tears. I struggled with every sinew, trying to flip him, dislodge him, pushing hard against his chest with my free hand.

He smirked as he stared down at me. "You've certainly got more spunk in you than Mary had, I give you that," he growled. "If I had the time ..." His eyes gleamed with desire. "But not today. Guess it's time for that early retirement I'd always hoped for. Maybe the Keys. Go fishing out on Islamorada."

He settled the knife firmly in his grasp, and his gaze hardened. "Stay still. It'll be easier for you. Never did like to see an animal suffer."

I arched against him, pushing with all my might, screaming out my desire to live. "Nooo!"

His blade came up, his gaze fixed on mine, and –

SLAM

A thick branch walloped Barry in the side of the head, throwing him off me, and his body collapsed in a pile of brush. Jason pulled me to my feet, swinging me around behind him, and then stood, attentive. His breath came in long heaves, sweat dripping from every pore of his body.

A whispering breeze danced through the dense oak leaves. A chickadee called out with its *chick-a-dee-dee-dee* in the far-off reaches. A white, fluffy cloud drifted lazily across a dense blue sky.

At last Jason's voice came in a low growl. "Stay here." He reseated the branch in his hand, then inched closer to Barry, one step at a time. The sprawled figure did not move. Jason dropped to one knee by his side, putting his hand to Barry's neck. A heartbeat passed, then two.

Jason's voice was hoarse with relief. "He's dead."

He turned to look at me, his eyes sweeping my body with attention. "Are you all right? Any serious injuries?"

I shook my head no, my eyes drawing to the slow throb of blood sliding down his chest. Then I was in his arms, shaking, and he held me close.

His voice was a murmur which I heard throughout my soul. "It's all right, my love. It's all right."

Chapter 31

I stepped out onto the back porch, the misty clouds and soft sky wrapping around me like a down blanket. I rolled out my lavender yoga mat, and my eyes went automatically to the left-hand post of the stairs. The railing was empty. No little tree frog waited there with blinking eyes to keep me company. I strove to rein in the sadness, to accept that this was simply part of the cycle of nature.

I glanced to the right-hand post.

There he was, his tiny body speckled with grey, his round gaze holding mine with contentment. It almost seemed that he was smiling at me, that these past few days had been a gallivant of unusual delight. Now he was back home, ready for a rest, ready to relax alongside me as I went through downward facing dog and warrior two.

My voice rose in delight. "Jason!"

He was at the back slider in a moment, and his eyes twinkled. "Let me guess. The tree frog is back."

I laughed. "How'd you guess?"

He made a waving motion of his hand. "What else would have you so happy?"

I moved to the front of my mat, smiled tenderly at my tiny friend, and then began. I twisted from side to side, allowing my arms to flap like empty coat sleeves. It was how I started each day, and the rhythm was smooth, soothing, awakening all of my senses. I'd heard this motion described as a "psychic washing machine," and I found that image fit as well as any other. It was a wringing loose, a shaking off, a releasing of the old.

It was the perfect way to begin.

* * *

Jason's trio had been slated to perform at the Blackstone National Golf Club for the evening, but it turned out Paul had been double-booked to play a clam bake out on Bourne and Meredith wanted to spend the weekend camping with Simel. So the gig had been turned over to Bret Talbert, a talented guitarist Paul had played with years ago.

We were inside the main dining area, due to the greying skies, and the atmosphere was bordering on raucous. The bar was chock full of people, and half the tables in our larger area were occupied as well. Derrick and Xander sat across from me and Jason as Bret belted out, "Sweet Caroliiiiiine –"

The crowd answered at the top of its lungs, "Ba Ba Baaaaa!"

I laughed, leaning against Jason. When the song wound to its end the room filled with applause and cheers.

Bret took a sip of his water, then nodded to Jason with a smile. "Now to slow things down a bit." He looked down at his strings, and in a moment his fingers were dancing through the gorgeous guitar intro to Zeppelin's "Over the Hills and Far Away."

I sighed with pleasure. It was one of my favorites.

Cheryl came by with a smile, placing a pair of chicken parms in front of me and Jason. "With veggies instead of pasta," she confirmed as she laid them down. She looked at me. "Another shiraz?"

I nodded. "That would be lovely."

She looked over at the other two. "You're all set?"

Xander nodded with a smile. "We had our steamers earlier, when we came in from our game."

She leant forward, pressing a kiss on his forehead. "You just let me know if you need anything."

He ran a hand along her cheek, his eyes shining, and she winked at him before heading back into the kitchen.

Derrick leant forward. "So Ephraim will recover?"

I took a sip of my wine. "He will indeed. He probably won't regain full use of his right arm, but the doctors were able to stabilize him."

Derrick turned to look at Jason. "And you. Fourteen stitches, huh?"

Jason's mouth quirked. "A mere scratch, compared with what some of my co-workers sport. I'm barely an entry in the 'impressive scars' contest that goes on in my field."

I put my hand on his. He looked over, and for a moment I was deep in the shadowed woods, Barry was swinging the blade, and Jason was falling … falling …

Jason's voice eased into a quieter tone. "I am all right," he murmured.

I twined my fingers into his and gave a wry smile. "I know."

Xander shook his head, sipping his Coke. "It's still hard to take in, that Barry would have done that to his own sister. I knew he had a temper; that's part of why I wanted to get her out of there. But I never would have guessed he'd go so far."

Jason nodded. "It was a crime of passion. Between him losing Mary to you, Cecily's tug-of-war games, and his obsession with courting that rich heiress, he had worked himself into a frenzy. He took Mary to that drive-in to reconnect, to reclaim some part of her for himself."

He gave a wry smile. "But she was too far gone. She had tasted freedom, and she would not be caged. They had words and fought. She ran into the woods to get away from him – and he pursued."

He looked down at our twined hands. "Barry insisted that she stop seeing you, Xander. She flat out refused. She vowed that she was going to marry you. And Barry …" Jason sighed. "Barry lost all reason. He attacked her, and the next thing he knew, she was dead."

Derrick's voice was a growl. "And Ephraim promptly covered up for him."

My voice was low. "Ephraim had already lost both of his parents. Now he'd lost his beloved younger sister. His younger brother was all he had left. He did his best to protect the only family member remaining." I gave a soft shrug. "I don't agree with it, but I can understand how hard it was for him."

Jason looked over. "And now Ephraim has, truly, lost everything. Barry's dead. With Ephraim's shoulder injury he'll have to give up his business as well. The D.A. won't be able to prosecute on accessory to murder, not with the lack of evidence, but there isn't much left for him."

I gave a soft smile. "He's talked with Cecily."

Jason raised an eyebrow. "Oh?"

"The moment he was out of surgery, he called her. He's setting up an exhibition of Mary's work. A celebration of her life and talents. He wants to set up funding to help artists who want to continue on with Mary's legacy – to help keep memory of the Holocaust victims alive. So we never forget."

His face eased at that. "That should give him a new purpose – and be a way for him to redeem himself."

Bret moved into Tom Petty's "American Girl," and I thought about the lyrics. The young woman craving something more. Mary had craved a better life for herself and Xander, and it had come crashing down on them both.

Cheryl came back over to the table with my wine, placing it before me. Then she laid her hand gently on Xander's shoulder, her eyes shining, moving her head in time with the music.

I looked to Jason and smiled. Healing was beginning. There would be scars, but the new skin would grow stronger, tougher, and the lives would go on. Mary's legacy would be celebrated.

Jason brought my fingers to his lips. His soft kiss echoed throughout my soul.

Dedication

Heart-felt thanks to:

Paul and Anne Holzwarth provided invaluable support and help in my research on Sutton's history.

Dave Furey, the forest ranger who inspired the Jason character when he passed me on his mountain bike on that first day in November 2012. I met with him during the writing of Birch Blackguards and learned a great deal about the duties and abilities of our rangers.

Sutton Police Chief Towle explained the details of police investigations and gave me a tour of the station, so I could ground my story with a solid foundation.

Gary Vaillancourt was kind enough to come in on a Saturday and provide a personalized tour of the Vaillancourt Folk Art workshop, including examining the original 1984 Santas.

Frank Robertson is a talented artist who works with both watercolors and acrylics. He provided critical details in helping me bring the artistic side of this story to life.

Neptune's Car is an amazing local band featuring the talented musicianship of Holly Hanson and Steve Hayes. Be sure to visit NeptunesCar.com to hear their music and support their efforts.

Sandra, Yvonne, Ruth, and Dad, who all provided wonderful feedback on the developing story. If I missed someone, please let me know!

Most of all, warm thanks to my darling partner Bob See of eighteen years and counting. Bob supports my dreams, encourages me in my projects, and is my foundation of strength.

Glossary

Higgins Armory – First opened in 1931, the Higgins Armory held about 2,000 pieces of armor, weaponry, and other historic material from all over the globe. In 2013 its funding ran dry, and it closed its doors on December 31, 2013. Its collection was handed over to the Worcester Art Museum.

Manchaug Pond – A 380-acre body of water in the southwest corner of Sutton, against the Douglas line. In 2013 a large, 100-acre plot of land on Manchaug was nearly sold for development. At the last moment an anonymous donor stepped forward with the $2 million necessary to keep the land pristine.

Singletary Lake – This lake is 330 acres and is partially in Sutton, partially in Millbury. Marion's Camp is on the Sutton side and is now the location of the town beach. The public boat ramp is on the northern, Millbury side.

Sutton Drive-In – Opened in 1947, the Sutton Drive-In is located on Route 146 South. It closed in August 1996 due to concerns about the traffic that backed up on 146 when cars were coming in. The screen, ticket booth, projection house, and large entry arch still remain.

Vaillancourt Folk Art – Founded in 1984 by Judi and Gary Vaillancourt, this artisan group creates fine collectible figurines out of chalkware made from antique candy molds. Each piece is created by hand in their workshop in Sutton, Massachusetts. The 1984 design is a real one, and Judi did originally experiment with beeswax. However, there was no version made for a commemoration event.

West End Creamery – Originally a dairy farm tracing back four generations, the current owners decided in 1987 to convert over to offering ice cream, a corn maze, miniature golf, and other family-friendly activities.

About the Author

Lisa Shea was born in Maryland during the Vietnam War to a father in the Air Force and a mother who worked as a journalist. She grew up in various towns along the eastern seaboard, raised in an environment where writing and researching the past were as natural as spending weekends tromping through old-growth woods looking for stone wall foundations. Her concept of art focused on cemetery stone rubbings and photos of old homesteads.

When Lisa moved to Sutton, Massachusetts in 1995, she finally found her true home. Sutton's rustic charm, dense forests, and bucolic farmland all resonated with her creative spirit. The stories she had been writing since she was young now had a fertile ground in which to flourish.

Lisa's first book set in Sutton, *Aspen Allegations*, was written in November 2012 in a chapter-a-day style. Each day she explored Sutton and its surrounding areas and then wrote those experiences into the chapter. The mystery-romance earned a gold medal from the 2013 IPPY awards. Her second book, *Birch Blackguards*, was written in the same chapter-a-day style in August 2013. The third book in the series will be written starting on May 1, 2014.

All proceeds from the Sutton Mass Mysteries series benefit local battered women's shelters.

Lisa Shea has written 21 fiction books and 67 non-fiction books.

About Birch Blackguards

Birch Blackguards is the second in a series of mystery novels set in Sutton Massachusetts. Information on this series can be found here –

http://suttonmass.org/suttonmassmysteries/

Birch Blackguards, just like the first novel *Aspen Allegations*, was written in "real time". Each day's chapter was first written on the actual day the events took place. Locations were visited and described as they appeared on that day.

Here's a photo of Renoir's painting *Jewish Wedding* that I took at the Worcester Art Museum on the day it's first mentioned in the story.

More photos of the locations described can be found at SuttonMass.org.

All proceeds from this series benefit a local domestic violence shelter.

Lisa Shea's library of medieval romance novels:

Each novel is a stand-alone story set in medieval England. These novels can be read in any order and have entirely separate casts of characters.

All proceeds from sales of these novels benefit battered women's shelters.

As a special treat, as a warm thank-you for buying this book and supporting the cause of battered women, here's a sneak peak at the first chapter of *Finding Peace – a Medieval Romance*.

Finding Peace was awarded a 2013 Silver Medal from the Independent Publisher Book Awards.

Finding Peace Chapter 1

England, 1212

"Anger is short-lived madness."
-- Horace

"God's Teeth, next the badgers and wolves will march by two-by-two," scowled Elizabeth with vehemence as she lugged the soaked saddle off her roan and dropped it in a sodden heap on the cracked bench. The fierce November storm crashed down all around her, hammering off the thin roof, reverberating through the small stable's walls. The lantern hanging in the corner guttered out dense smoke, barely holding off the deep gloom of the late hour.

She worked quickly in the flickering dark to bed down her horse, the familiar routine doing little to soothe her foul mood. She was drenched to the bone – her heavy cloak and hood had done little to shield her after the first ten minutes in the torrent. Her stomach was twisting into knots with hunger. Exhaustion and cold caused her fingers to fumble as she finished with the bridle. She hung it on the wooden peg, then turned to walk the few short steps toward the stable entrance.

The small inn's door was only ten steps away, but it seemed like ten miles through the deluge. Elizabeth took in a deep breath, pulled her hood up over her head, tucked in her glossy auburn curls, then sprinted across the dark cobblestones. It felt as if she were diving into a frigid stream, struggling against its strong current, and she reached out a hand for the thick, wooden door. In another second she had pulled open the latch, spun through the door, and slammed it heavily behind her.

The inn looked like every other hell hole she had stayed in during this long, tiring trip. Six or seven food-strewn oak tables filled the small space, about half occupied by aging farmers and rheumatic merchants. A doddering, wispy-haired barkeep poured ale behind a wood plank counter. The only two women in the room were a pair of buxom barmaids, one blonde, one redhead, laughing at a round table in the back with a trio of men. Two of the men appeared to be in their early twenties and were alike enough to be twins. Their dusty brown hair was the exact same color, the same periwinkle blue eyes gazed out from square faces. Like every other pair in the room, they swept up to stare at her the moment she came to rest, dripping from every seam, against the interior side of the door. After a moment of halfhearted interest, the farmers, merchants, and twins turned back to their pints of ale and their conversations on turnips and wool prices.

All except one. The third man, sitting somewhat apart from the preening twins and the flirtatious waitresses, held her gaze with steady interest. Her world slowed down, her skin tingled as a drip of water slid its way down her neck, tracing along every inch of her spine.

He was in his late twenties, a dark brown mane of hair curling just at his shoulders. He was well built, with the toned shoulders of a man who led an active life. It was his eyes that caught her and held her pinned against the wall. They were a rich moss green, a verdant color she remembered so strongly that her breath caught, her left hand almost swung down toward her hilt of its own accord.

She shook herself, turning to the row of wooden pegs running in an uneven line next to the door. That man was in the past, and by God, he would stay there. Why did she have to keep seeing that foul bastard's eyes everywhere, in every tavern, in every stranger she passed on the road? She pushed the hood of her cloak back, then shook its damp embrace off her body, revealing the simple, burnt-orange dress she wore beneath and the well-used sword hanging on her right hip.

Now, to get some stew, or gruel, or whatever mystery meat this cook had to offer, and get some sleep.

"You, woman!" came the growled order, plunging the room into immediate silence.

Elizabeth blew out her breath in an exasperated huff. Just for once she would like to have her food and rest without going through this ordeal. Sometimes it was just a snide comment, a mention of the dangers of a young woman traveling alone, or a sly joke about the "oldest profession". Sometimes the greeting cut with its chill edge. One solemn innkeeper had served her meal brusquely, informing her that she would have to find somewhere else to sleep.

All she wanted was food and a bed. She took in a deep breath and closed her eyes for a moment. If she could just rein in her temper she could get through this and snatch a few hours' reprieve from the torrential deluge.

She turned around slowly, holding her features in what she hoped was a neutral gaze. The twins were on their feet, their eyes sharp on her, their faces twisted in anger. They wore matching outfits of fine leather jerkins. Behind them the green-eyed man stood more slowly, his eyes scanning her with careful attention.

Twin number one shouted in rage. "You! Woman! I cannot believe you simply strolled in here and expect to be fed and cared for!" His eyes nearly bulged from their sockets. "What, did you expect a pint of ale?"

Elizabeth blinked in surprise. She had certainly encountered people in rural towns who thought little of her traveling alone – but she had reached new lows in hospitality with this outpost from Hades. Still, the hammering of the torrential downpour just outside the door encouraged her to press her case.

"Please," she bit out, her rising anger sharpening the edges of her attempted civility, "all I want is something hot to eat and a place to sleep. In the morning I will be out of your town and on my way."

Twin number two took a step forward. "Maybe you did not hear my brother, John," he snarled, his voice perhaps even a few notes higher than his double. "I think we should step outside."

His brother's voice was almost like hearing an echo. "Absolutely, Ron," agreed the clone with heat.

Elizabeth couldn't help herself. John and Ron. Twins. The rhyming duo. Her laughter bubbled up within her, emerging from her exhaustion, her frustration, her hunger and weariness with the world. It was the final straw in the long carnival which had made up these past few weeks.

The brothers glanced at each other, fury boiled their faces crimson, and her left hand dropped to her hip, doing the twist – latch – release to free her sword hilt from its clasp in one smooth movement. She had her weapon sliding smoothly from its sheath in the same moment that the pair launched themselves across the spellbound tavern toward her. Her steel rose in an arcing block as John brought a haymaker drive down toward her skull. She deflected his blow easily, sliding it off to her left, turning and whipping the sword – flat first – against his kidney with the full force of her momentum. He screamed in pain and sprawled back on the rough wooden floor, his face contorted in agony.

She continued her spin, remaining low, the whistle of Ron's blade skimming over her head. She kicked her boot hard against his kneecap. He buckled backwards, screaming in fury, and she rose, whirling her sword in a circular motion, preparing to give him a welt to remember her by.

There was a dark figure before her. Her moving blade slammed into a block, was held, and she looked up into moss green eyes. Her breath caught, and she leant her sword against the tension. Her blade pressed in an X against his, their hands nearly touching, his body presenting a barrier now between her and the two young men.

"My name is Richard." His voice rumbled out deep, steady, serious. He gazed at her face for a long minute. "I would call your eyes a deep brown, would you agree?"

Elizabeth shook her head in confusion. "What? I suppose," she ground out, continuing her press against his sword. The man had excellent balance; his arm did not move one breath.

Richard turned his head slightly, calling down to the two at his feet. "Certainly not ice blue," he informed them calmly.

His focus came back to her. "I apologize for these two impetuous ones, and would ask that you choose to stay at the Traveler's Inn, a scant mile east. To be truthful, they are much cleaner than this location."

A hot flare of fury burst through her. She was attacked, and now she was the one who had to leave? It was the second coming of the Flood out there! She snapped her sword free of his and sidestepped to the right, determined to finish what she had started.

Richard moved easily with her, brought his sword hilt back against his hip, and pointed the tip between her eyes. His body remained evenly between hers and the sprawled men. "I will defend them," he added in a cool, steady voice. Elizabeth could see the steel settle into his gaze. She remembered being sheltered by that same style of fierce protectiveness, remembered being sprawled, herself, on a cold floor, her guardian angel standing resolutely between her and danger.

God's teeth, she missed her brother.

The burning flame of fury ebbed within her, and she sighed. It was not worth it, not for a flea-bitten mat in this God forsaken hole in the ground.

She took a step back, slid her sword smoothly back into its sheath, then turned on her heel. She pulled the soaking wet cloak over her shoulders, shivering as its damp caress sucked the warmth out of her body. She half kicked the door open. Outside the rain pummeled the ground as if to beat it into submission, and she nearly turned back, nearly took on all three.

"Here," came a call behind her. She turned, and Richard tossed her two golden coins. She caught them easily as they came near her, and the corner of his mouth twitched up in appreciation.

Now she was being paid to leave. She turned back toward the rain, took a deep breath, and walked steadfastly into the torrent, leaving the door wide open behind her.

Here's where to learn what happened next!

Finding Peace
http://www.lisashea.com/medievalromance/findingpeace/

Thank you so much for all of your support and encouragement for this important cause.

Made in the USA
San Bernardino, CA
10 May 2014